Praise for *The Seventh* and Ric

"[T]he non-hero: the ruthless, ￼
erator in a humorless and amc￼ ...￼o one depicts
this scene with greater clarity than Richard Stark."
                    —Allen J. Rubin, *New York Times Book Review*

"Richard Stark's Parker . . . is refreshingly amoral, a thief who
always gets away with the swag."
                    —Stephen King, *Entertainment Weekly*

"Donald E. Westlake (who writes as Richard Stark when he
wants to see how far he can push it) has a wonderfully twisted
mind that takes impish delight in knocking over its own elabo-
rate plot constructions."
                    —Marilyn Stasio, *New York Times Book Review*

"Westlake's ability to construct an action story filled with un-
foreseen twists and quadruple-crosses is unparalleled."
                    —*San Francisco Chronicle*

"The Parker novels . . . are among the greatest hard-boiled
writing of all time."
                    —*Financial Times* (London)

"Richard Stark's Parker novels, a cluster of which were written
in an extraordinary burst of creativity in the early '60s, are
among the most poised and polished fictions of their time and,
in fact, of any time."
                    —John Banville, *Bookforum*

The Seventh

Parker Novels By Richard Stark

The Hunter (Payback)

The Man with the Getaway Face

The Outfit

The Mourner

The Score

The Jugger

The Seventh

The Handle

The Rare Coin Score

The Green Eagle Score

The Black Ice Score

The Sour Lemon Score

Deadly Edge

Slayground

Plunder Squad

Butcher's Moon

Comeback

Backflash

Flashfire

Firebreak

Breakout

Nobody Runs Forever

Ask the Parrot

Dirty Money

The Seventh

RICHARD STARK

With a New Foreword by Luc Sante

The University of Chicago Press

The University of Chicago Press, Chicago 60637
© 1966 by Richard Stark
Foreword © 2009 by Luc Sante
All rights reserved.
University of Chicago Press edition 2009

Printed in the United States of America

20 19 18 17 16 15 14 13 12   4 5 6 7

ISBN-13: 978-0-226-77105-2 (paper)
ISBN-10: 0-226-77105-9 (paper)

Library of Congress Cataloging-in-Publication Data

Stark, Richard, 1933–2008.
 The seventh / Richard Stark ; with a new foreword by Luc Sante.
     p. cm.
 Originally published under title: The split.
 Summary: The seventh book in the Parker series, this describes the aftermath of a
brilliant heist at a college football game.
  ISBN-13: 978-0-226-77105-2 (pbk. : alk. paper)
  ISBN-10: 0-226-77105-9 (pbk. : alk. paper) 1. Parker (Fictitious character)—
Fiction. 2. Criminals—Fiction. I. Sante, Luc. II. Title.
 PS3573.E9S48 2009
 813'.54—dc22

                                                                    2009006775

♾ The paper used in this publication meets the minimum requirements of the
American National Standard for Information Sciences—Permanence of Paper for
Printed Library Materials, ANSI Z39.48-1992.

Foreword

THE PARKER novels by Richard Stark are a singularly long-lasting literary franchise, established in 1962 and pursued to the present, albeit with a twenty-three-year hiatus in the middle. In other ways, too, they are a unique proposition. When I read my first Parker novel—picked up at random, and in French translation, no less—I was a teenager, and hadn't read much crime fiction beyond Sherlock Holmes and Agatha Christie. I was stunned by the book, by its power and economy and the fact that it blithely dispensed with moral judgment, and of course I wanted more. Not only did I want more Parker and more Stark, I also imagined that I had stumbled upon a particularly brilliant specimen of a thriving genre. But I was wrong. There is no such genre.

To be sure, there are plenty of tight, harsh crime novels, beginning with Dashiell Hammett's *Red Harvest,* and there is a substantial body of books written from the point of view of the criminal, ranging from the tortured cries of Jim Thompson and David Goodis to the mordantly analytical *romans durs* by Georges Simenon. There are quite a few caper novels, including the comic misadventures Parker's creator writes under his real name, Donald Westlake, and the works of a whole troop of French writers not well known in this country: José Giovanni, Albert Simonin, San-Antonio. The lean, efficient Giovanni in particular has points in common with Stark (Anglophones can best approach him through movie adaptations: Jean-

Pierre Melville's *Le deuxième souffle,* Claude Sautet's *Classe tous risques*), but with the key difference that Giovanni is an unabashed romantic.

Stark is not a romantic, or at least not within the first six feet down from the surface. Westlake has said that he meant the books to be about "a workman at work," which they are, and that is why they have so few useful parallels, why they are virtually a genre unto themselves. Process and mechanics and troubleshooting dominate the books, determine their plots, underlie their aesthetics and their moral structure. A great many of the editions down through the years have prominently featured a blurb from Anthony Boucher: "Nobody tops Stark in his objective portrayal of a world of total amorality." That is true as far as it goes—it is never suggested in the novels that robbing payrolls or shooting people who present liabilities are anything more than business practices—but Boucher overlooked the fact that Parker maintains his own very lively set of moral prerogatives. Parker abhors waste, sloth, frivolity, inconstancy, double-dealing, and reckless endangerment as much as any Puritan. He hates dishonesty with a passion, although you and he may differ on its terms. He is a craftsman who takes pride in his work.

Parker is in fact a bit like the ideal author of a crime-fiction series: solid, dependable, attentive to every nuance and detail. He is annoyed by small talk and gets straight to the point in every instance, using no more than the necessary number of words to achieve his aim. He eschews shortcuts, although he can make difficult processes look easy, and he is free of any trace of sentiment, although he knows that while planning and method and structure are crucial, character is even more important. As brilliant as he is as a strategist, he is nothing short of phenomenal at instantly grasping character. This means that he sometimes sounds more like a fictional detective than a crook, but mostly he sounds like a writer. In order to decide which path the double-crosser he is pursuing is most likely to have taken, or which member of the string is most likely to double-cross, or the odds on a reasonable-sounding job that has just been proposed to him by someone with shaky credentials, he has to get all the way under the skin of the party in question. He is an exceptionally intelligent freelancer in a risky profession who takes on difficult jobs hoping for a payoff large enough to hold off the next job for as long as possible. He even has an agent (Joe Sheer succeeded by Handy McKay). Then again he is seen—by other characters as well as readers—as lacking in emotion, let alone sympathy, a thug whose sole motivation is self-interest.

And no wonder: Parker is a big, tough man with cold eyes. "His hands looked like they'd been molded of brown clay by a sculptor who thought big and liked veins"; the sentence appears like a Homeric epithet somewhere in an early chapter of most of the books. He might just possibly pass for a businessman, provided the business is something like used cars or jukeboxes. He doesn't drink much, doesn't gamble, doesn't read, likes to sit in the dark, thinking, or else in front of the television, not watching but employing it as an aid to concentration. Crude and antisocial at the start of the series, he actually evolves considerably over its course. Claire, whom he meets in *The Rare Coin Score*, seems to have a lot to do with this—by *Deadly Edge* they actually have a house together. And Alan Grofield, first encountered in *The Score* and recurring in *The Handle*, among other titles, twice in the series becomes the recipient of what can only be called acts of kindness from Parker, however much Stark equivocates on this point, insisting that they merely reflect professional ethics or some such.

Parker is a sort of supercriminal—not at all like those European master criminals, such as Fantômas and Dr. Mabuse, but a very American freebooter, able to outmaneuver the Mob, the CIA, and whatever other forces come at him. For all that he lives on the other side of the law, he bears a certain resemblance to popular avengers of the 1960s and '70s, Dirty Harry or Charles Bronson's character in *Death Wish*. He is a bit of a fanatic, and even though we are repeatedly told how sybaritic his off duty resort-hotel lifestyle is, it remains hard to picture, since he is such an ascetic in the course of the stories. He is so utterly consumed by the requirements of his profession that everything extraneous to it is suppressed when he's on, and we are not privy to his time off, except for narrow vignettes in which he is glimpsed having sex or, once, swimming. But then, writers are writing even when they're not writing, aren't they?

After *The Hunter,* all the remaining titles concern jobs gone wrong, which seems to be the case for most of Parker's jobs, barring the occasional fleeting allusion to smoother operations in the past. *The Seventh* is, naturally, the seventh book in the series, as well as a reference to the split from the take in a stadium job. The actual operation is successful; the problem is what occurs afterward. It represents the very rare incursion, for the Parker series, of a thriller staple: the crazed gunman. Along with *The Rare Coin Score,* it is one of Stark's always verypointed explorations of group dynamics. *The Handle,* with its private gambling island, ex-Nazi villain, and international intrigue, is (like *The Mourner* and *The Black Ice Score*) a nod to the espionage craze of the 1960s, when authors of thrillers could not afford to ignore James Bond. If *The Seventh* is primarily aftermath, *The Handle* is largely preamble. In *The Rare Coin Score* (the first of four such titles, succeeded by *Green Eagle, Black Ice, and Sour Lemon*) the culprit is an amateur, a coin dealer whose arrested development is so convincingly depicted the reader can virtually hear his voice squeak. Sharp characterizations abound in this one—its plot turns entirely on character flaws of various sizes.

The Parker books are all engines, machines that start up with varying levels of difficulty, then run through a process until they are done, although subject to different sorts of interference. The heists depicted are only part of this process—sometimes they are even peripheral to it. Parker is the mechanic who runs the machine and attempts to keep it oiled and on course. The interference is always caused by personalities—by the greed, incompetence, treachery, duplicity, or insanity of individuals concerned, although this plays out in a variety of ways, depending on whether it affects the job at beginning, middle, or end, and whether it occurs as a single dramatic action, a domino sequence of contingencies, or a gradually fraying rope. The beauty of the machine is that not only does it allow for the usual suspense, but it also maximizes the effectiveness of its opposite: the satisfaction of inevitability. Some Parker novels are fantastically intricate clockwork mechanisms (*The Hunter, The Outfit,* the seemingly unstoppable *Slayground,* the epic *Butcher's Moon*), while others hurtle along as successions of breakdowns (the aptly acidic *The Sour Lemon Score,* the almost sadistically frustrating *Plunder Squad*). Like all machines but unlike lesser thrillers the novels have numerous moving parts, and the more the better—more people, more subplots, more businesslike detail, more glimpses of marginal lives. Stark's momentum is such that the more matter he throws into the hopper the faster the gears turn. The books are machines that all but read themselves. You can read the entire series and not once have to invest in a bookmark.

Luc Sante
December 2008

The Seventh

PART ONE

1

When he didn't get any answer the second time he knocked, Parker kicked the door in. Only the cheap bolt lock was fastened; the chain lock and the police lock were both open. Parker raised his foot and kicked the flat of his shoe against the door above the knob just one time, and the door popped open like it was surprised. It went with a dry cracking sound as pieces of doorframe ripped away from around the bolt. It was dry old wood in a rotten old building and it split easy.

The door swung all the way open, the inner knob bumping finally against the side wall, but Parker didn't go in right away. He stood in the hall, under the twenty-five-watt bulb stuck in the ceiling, and waited and listened.

The door stood open on a long narrow hall. All the rooms of the apartment opened off that hall, to the right. The kitchen was first, with light spilling out the doorway. Next was the bathroom, in darkness, that part of the hall dark also. Next the bedroom, soft light spreading out to the hallway from there. Last was the living-room, into which the hallway emptied. From out here on the other side of the apartment doorway Parker could look down the hall like looking down a long rectangular funnel and see an edge of the living-room at the far end, a dark brown mohair overstuffed armchair and a rickety dark wood table with a black telephone on it and the beginning of an imitation Persian rug. Also a floor lamp, standing beyond the armchair, lit now and making a soft glow out around its cream shade. There was another light source too, deeper in the living room, out of sight.

Everything the way he'd left it. Light on in the kitchen, off in the bathroom, on in the bedroom and living-room. Bolt lock fastened on the front door, chain lock and police lock both unfastened. Everything the way he'd left it.

Except he'd knocked twice just now and Ellie hadn't come to open the door.

He'd gone downstairs ten minutes ago, to buy beer and cigarettes. The place on the corner was closed and he'd walked a block farther to the next place, and now he was back.

Ordinarily he'd have sent Ellie, but he hadn't been out of the apartment in three days and he felt like having some fresh air. So he dressed, while she sat on the rumpled bed nude, cross-legged tailor fashion, smoking a filter cigarette and scratching herself. She kept yawning, but the yawns that come after sleep, not before. "I'll make us some eggs," she offered, and he said: "Fine," and then he left.

And now, in ten minutes, something had managed to go wrong.

She wouldn't have gone out. And she wouldn't have gone back to sleep. She should have heard him knock, and even if she hadn't she sure as hell should have heard him kick the door in.

There was nothing in the apartment but silence.

Parker felt naked standing out here under this twenty-five watt bulb, wearing nothing but clothes. He had no weapon —nothing but a bag with beer bottles and cigarette packages in it.

He put the paper bag down on the floor and reached just inside the doorway and around the other side of the split doorframe to where he'd leaned the bar of the police lock when he'd gone out. His fingers closed on it, and it was cold. He picked it up and stood hefting it. It was good iron, solid, three feet long. When it was in operation, one end was stuck at a slant into the metal plate in the floor behind the door, the other end in the locking mechanism on the door itself. With this bar wedged between door and floor, nobody would kick the door in; police lock was a good name for it.

8

It would make a good weapon. Better than bare hands.

Parker stepped across the threshold and shut the door behind him. It wouldn't shut all the way anymore. The hall was bright near to him, where light spilled out from the kitchen, and then dim farther on and softly glowing down at the living-room end.

Parker moved noiselessly forward and looked into the kitchen. It was three inches bigger than a closet and filled with appliances. A white circular fluorescent light fixture meant for a room of normal size glared in the middle of the ceiling, reflecting balefully from all the porcelain and white enamel crowded into the little room. Dirty glasses, dirty pots, dirty dishes, were scattered all over every flat surface. Grocery bags full of rubbish were crammed together on the floor.

No eggs had been started. Ellie wasn't in this room now, and it didn't look as though she'd been here at all.

Parker moved on and switched on the bathroom light, and this room, too, was empty. He left the light on and went past there and when he got even with the bedroom doorway he looked in and she was sitting there on the bed.

At first he didn't see the hilt, and he thought she'd just fallen asleep again.

She was sitting there just the same as when he'd left, legs crossed tailor fashion, back against the headboard of the bed, arms at her sides. A faint wisp of smoke was coming up from the area of her left hand, so she was still smoking the cigarette. Or had started a new one by now.

The only difference he saw at first was she wasn't looking up. Her head was slumped forward as though she'd fallen asleep again. Except the position looked awkward; it looked as though if she were asleep she'd fall over frontward. He looked at her from the hallway, frowning, the picture looking wrong, not understanding why yet, and then he saw the hilt jutting out from between her breasts.

Somebody had taken one of the crossed swords from the wall and jammed it through her chest and through the padded headboard of the bed and into the plasterboard of the wall. She was stuck there like a scarecrow put away for the winter.

9

The guy who did it had a hell of an arm. Either that, or he'd brought a sledge along to hammer it the rest of the way after the first thrust.

Parker moved deeper into the room, looking around, but there was nobody here now. The guy had been and gone.

There was practically no blood visible at all. It must have mostly gone out the back and soaked into the headboard padding.

So what now? He was supposed to stay here two more days. If he left, the others wouldn't know where to get in touch with him, and he didn't know where to get in touch with them, not easily. But he couldn't stick around with that thing on the bed.

Ten minutes. That was awfully damn fast. The guy must have been watching the place, waiting for Parker to get out of the way. As soon as Parker left, in he came, and right back out again.

Parker wondered what Ellie had done to somebody to make him that irritated with her. He'd only known her two weeks himself, and neither of them had spent much time on autobiography. This was her apartment, and he'd guessed that she'd inherited it from a man, that she'd originally lived here with somebody. The crossed swords on the wall, the beer mugs on the mantel in the living room, the round table in a corner of the living room that must have been used at one time for poker sessions, all told of a male presence here. Probably either a college boy or somebody who wished he still was a college boy.

Maybe it was the college boy who'd done it. A football hero, maybe, offensive lineman, with the meaty shoulders and blunt strength needed to wield that damn sword that way.

But it didn't matter. Parker didn't give a damn who'd killed her, or why. It aggravated him because his plans were loused up now. He had no choice; he had to get out of here.

He turned and saw Mutt and Jeff standing in the doorway, wearing rumpled police uniforms. Mutt looked surprised, as though somebody had played a dirty trick on him, and Jeff looked frightened. They were both reaching for their pistols with a clumsy haste that would have made their old instructor at the Police Academy break down and cry.

The public cries for a bigger police force and after a while any damn fool can join up if he's only tall enough.

Parker said, "That was fast. I just called a minute ago."

Mutt stopped where he was, but Jeff kept on tugging and actually got his revolver out in his hand. He pointed it about two feet to Parker's left and said, "Don't move."

Mutt told him, "Hold on a minute." To Parker he said, "You're the one phoned in?"

"Sure." Parker put an agreeable smile on his face, but he didn't feel agreeable. So the guy had come in here, killed her, waited till Parker had gone back in, and then called the cops, figuring Parker was his patsy.

He could figure again. Parker said, "I'm the one called."

"How come you wouldn't give your name?" Mutt was frowning all around his nose.

Parker shrugged. "Why waste the time? I was going to stick around here anyway."

Jeff spoke again. "It don't smell right," he told his partner.

Mutt said, "We'll see." He dragged a flat black note-book out of his pocket and flipped it open like he planned to give Parker a ticket. The notebook came with its own pencil, stuck in a little loop at the side. Mutt slid the pencil out, poised it, looked at his watch, wrote down the time, and said to Parker, "Tell me about it."

"I went out to get beer and cigarettes. I left it out in the hall there; you probably saw the bag."

Mutt nodded, but Jeff made an obvious effort to show a poker face. He wasn't giving anything away, Jeff wasn't.

Parker said, "When I came back I knocked on the door, and when I didn't get any answer I knew something was wrong."

Jeff, the sharpie, said, "How?"

Parker looked at him. "Because she was in here and all right when I left, and I was gone ten minutes, and there wasn't any reason for her not to be in here and all right when I got back. If she didn't hear me knock on the door, that meant there was something wrong."

Jeff waggled the gun in a gesture that was supposed to be airy. "Go on," he said.

Parker said, "I knocked twice, and then I kicked the door in. I came in here and saw her like that and phoned for you guys. Then I waited."

Mutt looked at his partner. "It *sounds* okay," he said.

Jeff wasn't so sure anymore. He said to Parker, "You search the place?"

"Not the living room. I only got as far as here."

"Watch him," Jeff told his partner, and took his gun away to go search the living room.

While Jeff was gone, Mutt apologized for him, saying to Parker, "Don't mind him. He's new on the force."

"Sure."

Parker was distracted, trying to figure a graceful way out of here. He could only sweet-talk these cops for so long, and then it didn't matter if they were stupid or not. Anybody in the vicinity of a crime, innocent or guilty, is going to be asked questions, routine questions about name and residence and occupation and what are you doing here now, and there wasn't a question those cops could ask that Parker would be able to answer.

He had to ditch them. He had to get his goods and clear out of here.

Jeff came back and shook his head at his partner. He actually thought he was Humphrey Bogart.

Mutt said, "We better phone in."

Jeff said, "What about the closet?"

"I looked in there," Parker told him. "It's empty."

"You never can tell," Jeff said. "Sometimes a man can hide in among the clothing; you won't even see him there."

Parker shook his head. "There's nobody in there."

"I'll take a look."

Parker watched him, cursing him. He'd open the door to the closet, and he'd see the guns and the suitcases full of money, and that would be the end of it. Parker backed up to the dresser.

Jeff opened the door and looked in and said, "What the hell is this? *Machine* guns!"

Parker picked the wooden jewelry box off the dresser and threw it at the back of Jeff's head. Before it landed, Parker had taken a quick step and drop-kicked Mutt into the wall. Mutt bounced back, holding his stomach, and Parker clubbed him across the jaw with a hard right and turned to see how Jeff was doing.

Jeff was being comical, without trying. The jewelry box had hit him in the back of the head and driven him into the closet, where his head and arms had got mixed up with the clothing hanging there and his feet had got tangled up with shoes and guns. He was backing out of it all now, shouting something that was muffled by the clothing all around his head. He'd dropped his own gun when he'd been hit, and it was down on the floor now with the others.

Parker went over there fast, pulled him the rest of the way out of the closet, turned him around, and hit him twice. Jeff fell back into the closet and crumpled.

Everything was a mess. Parker grabbed Jeff's feet and dragged him out of the closet so he could get at his goods. The two machine guns and four pistols were all rattling around together on the closet floor.

Parker cleared everything out of the way, and looked around inside the closet, and the suitcases full of money weren't there any more.

All right. So it wasn't somebody after Ellie, it was somebody after the money, and killing Ellie was just incidental. It was a double-cross from somebody else in on the heist, it had to be; nobody else could have known about the money. One of the others wanted the whole pie for himself, and figured to put Parker in a sling at the same time.

Not hardly. Parker filled his pockets with pistols, and left the apartment.

13

2

Parker walked across the blacktop past the gas pumps on their little concrete island. The pumps were bathed in light, spilling on Parker as he went by with his arms swinging from his shoulders like lethal weights. He was big and shaggy in the white light, with flat square shoulders and long muscle-roped arms. His hands looked like they'd been molded of brown clay by a sculptor who thought big and liked veins. He wore no hat; his dry brown hair fluttered on his skull, blown about by a cold November wind. He wore a dark gray suit and a black topcoat. His hands held pistols in the topcoat pockets.

The gas-station office was lit up just as much as the pumps. Inside, a chubby guy in a blue jumper was asleep at a metal desk. Parker walked on by the office and down into the darker area, down to the long shedlike building that took up the rest of the block. The entrance was a small door inset in a large corrugated sliding garage door; Parker pushed it open and stepped over the strip across the bottom.

It was past midnight by now, so the interior was more than half full of cabs gleaming yellow and red under the bare bulbs spaced along the ceilings. In the daytime this place would be as empty as an airplane hangar.

Over to the right a wooden shed with glass windows all around had been built into a corner. A guy in a mackinaw lay stretched out asleep on a bench outside this shed, and inside, through the windows, Parker could see two guys working at desks. They wore white shirts, but they'd loosened their ties and unbuttoned their shirt collars.

Parker walked across the concrete floor and pushed the shed door open and went in. One of the white-collar workers looked up and said, "Not here, buddy. You want to go outside and around to the front. The gas-station office is over there."

Parker kept his hands out of his topcoat pockets. He said, "I don't want the gas-station office."

The worker shook his head. "You don't want us either, pal. You got a problem, talk to the day workers."

"I'm looking for one of your drivers."

The other worker looked up, interested. The first one said, "Which one?"

"Dan Kifka."

The worker frowned, and looked at his partner. "Kifka? You know any Kifka?"

The other one nodded. "Yeah. He works part-time, night-shift. He ain't been around for a month or more."

Parker said, "He's supposed to be working tonight."

The second worker shrugged and said, "I'll check it for you, but I'm pretty sure he ain't around." He got to his feet and went over to a table with small filing cabinets on it.

Parker waited, frowning. Kifka should be working tonight. And he should have been working last night and the night before. That was the cover, that kept him clean so he could stay out in the open.

If he wasn't working tonight, maybe it was because he was busy someplace else. Busy with swords, maybe.

The worker shut the file drawer and shook his head. "No, he ain't on tonight. It's been a month since he's been around here. Over a month."

"That's bad news," Parker said. He turned and went out.

There were no cabs running in this part of town—no reason for them. All the cabs here were parked inside garages. Parker started walking toward downtown.

He went two blocks, and then behind him a ways a voice called out, "Hey!" It had that odd strained sound a voice has when somebody tries to shout quietly.

Parker turned and saw a bulky man coming down the

sidewalk toward him. He moved past a streetlight as Parker watched, and it was the guy in the mackinaw, the one that had been asleep on the bench back in the cab garage. Parker put his right hand in his topcoat pocket, and stepped back into darker shadow in the lee of a tenement stoop.

They had this block to themselves. The windows of all the tenements on both sides were marked with the white X of urban renewal; they stood nearly empty, waiting for the wreckers. Within them the cockroaches crawled and the rats chittered, but the humans were away, infesting some other neighborhood. Outside, the street was empty of cars, either moving or parked. Except for the man in the mackinaw, nothing living moved on the sidewalk.

The man in the mackinaw hurried the last half block separating them, and then abruptly slowed and came forward more warily, head craned forward like a periscope, turning slowly from side to side. In a shrill whisper he called, "Where are you? Where'd you get to?"

"Here."

He stopped. "What are you doing? Come on out of there."

Parker said, "You want to talk, talk."

"You was asking about Dan Kifka."

"So?"

He hesitated, didn't seem to know how to go on. "Why don't you come out where I can see you?" He sounded plaintive.

Parker told him, "Say what you've got to say."

"You a friend of Kifka's?"

"In a way."

"He was supposed to be in tonight. Three nights in a row he was supposed to be in and he didn't show up."

"So I heard."

"They didn't tell you everything, back to the office. He keeps calling in sick. Every day he calls in sick and says be sure and leave him a slot for tomorrow, he'll be in for sure."

That didn't make any sense yet. Parker ignored it, and said, "What's your interest?"

"He owes me thirty-seven dollars for over a year now." The aggrieved tone wasn't faked; Parker relaxed a little.

Still, he said, "Why follow me?"

"I figured maybe you know where he is, maybe he owes you money, too, or something like that, and we can go see him together."

"You don't know where he lives?"

He hesitated again, and scuffed his feet on the sidewalk, and finally said, "No, I don't." This time he was obviously lying. The truth probably was he was afraid of Kifka, wouldn't dare brace Kifka alone in Kifka's apartment. That's why he'd been hanging around in the garage where there'd be other people there to help him in case Kifka got mad. And now he figured to ride along on Parker's coat-tails, but he was making a mistake.

Parker stepped out onto the sidewalk. "Forget it," he said.

"We can go see him together." He was pleading now. "Two heads are better than one," he said.

"Not always." Parker turned away and walked on. Ahead, far down the street, the world was more brightly lit. There he could find a cab to take him to Kifka's place.

The clown in the mackinaw wouldn't give up. He came padding along saying, "You're going to see him anyway, what difference does it make to you? I won't get in your way; I just want to get my thirty-seven bucks."

Parker stopped and turned around and said, "Walk someplace else."

"You don't have to be so goddam tough about it." He spoke with the whine of the natural loser, but he wouldn't give ground. He just stood there, unable to force himself on Parker and unwilling to go away and forget it.

Parker had no patience for this kind of clown. He took his hands out of his topcoat pockets, empty, and balled them into fists. He took a step toward the clown, but he skittered away like an underfed mongrel. Parker said, "Don't follow me."

The clown said, "It's a free country. I can walk where I want." He was at least forty years old, but he talked like a kid in a schoolyard.

Parker felt the pistols weighing heavy in his pockets, but that was no good. That answer was always too simple, too easy, and left the worst kind of trail. It was a temptation to be resisted.

17

Instead, he said to the clown, "I don't want you around." He let it go at that, and turned away, and walked on toward downtown.

The clown kept trailing along about a block behind.

Another three blocks and Parker was beginning to come into a more active section. He saw a cruising cab with its dome light lit, and stepped off the sidewalk to motion at it. The cab made a U-turn and stopped in front of him. He got into the back seat and gave Kifka's home address. The cabby pushed flag and accelerator down at the same time.

Looking out the rear window, Parker saw the clown standing there two blocks back, standing on the curb with his hands in his mackinaw pockets, his shoulders hunched as he gazed after the cab. He just stood there.

3

The blonde that opened the door had put on the first piece of clothing she'd come across, a gray sweatshirt with a picture of Bach on it. With one hand she was pulling it down in front, which meant she probably wasn't wearing pants either; it was obvious she wasn't wearing a bra.

Parker told her, "I want to see Dan."

"He's taking a nap," she said. She was about nineteen or twenty, looked like a college girl. Cheerleader type. Except she looked like a cheerleader who'd been on a binge, hair tousled, face puffy, eyes heavy-lidded, expression lethargic and sated.

Parker pushed the door the rest of the way open and went on into the apartment. "He'll want to see me," he said. "When he knows I'm here he'll want to wake up."

She couldn't give him her full attention, both because she was still half asleep and because she was having trouble keeping the sweatshirt on as much of her as she wanted. What with her breasts pushing outward and her hand pulling downward, Bach didn't look much like his old self at all.

She said, "You shouldn't push your way into places like that. I told you, Dan's taking a nap. He needs his rest."

"I'm sure he does."

"That isn't what I meant," she said. "I mean he's sick. He's got a virus."

"Fine." Parker had been here only once before, and then only in this living room, never deeper in the apartment. Now he looked around, saw two doors either of which could lead to the bedroom, and pointed at them, saying, 'Which one?"

"I don't want you to wake him,"she said, trying to sound like a private nurse. It might have come off better if she hadn't been out of uniform.

"I'm in a hurry," Parker told her. He took a pistol out of his right topcoat pocket, just to have it handy, because Kifka might be the one he was after.

She looked at it and her eyes went wide and she said, "What are you going to do to him?"

"Nothing. Where is he?"

"Please—Mister. . . . "

Parker shook his head. "I'm not going to do anything to him." He shut the hall door and walked over to the nearest of the two doors and opened it and looked in at a kitchen. He closed it again and went over to the other one and opened it, and this was the bedroom.

Kifka was there, sprawled across the bed like a dead horse. He was a big, blond hunky, built like an out-of-condition wrestler. He was apparently sleeping nude, with a wrinkled sheet half twisted around his body. From the look of him and the bed, he thrashed a lot in his sleep. If the blonde had been sharing the same bed with him, it had to be true love.

The bed was an old-fashioned double, with brass headboard and footboard like cell windows. Parker went over to the foot of the bed, seeing the clothing scattered all around the room like used snakeskins on a hot rock, and rapped the gun barrel against the brass footboard. The sound rang out in the room with surprising volume.

Kifka snorted and shifted around some on the bed. But he didn't wake up.

Then the girl, from the doorway, cried out, "Look out, Dan, he's got a gun!"

Kifka dove off the bed, lunging for a pile of clothing on the chair.

Parker said, "Dan! Hold it!"

Kifka was a tumbler. He landed on a shoulder, rolled, reversed, and came up on his feet. He was as naked as a piece of granite, with a red, sleepy, baffled face. He said, "What goes on? What the hell goes on?" From the sound of his voice, his head was stuffed with virus from ear to ear.

Parker told him, "We've got to talk, Dan."

"Parker?" Kifka frowned heavily and scrubbed his face with meaty palms. "This goddam virus won't get the hell out of here," he said.

The girl said, "Get back in bed, Dan, you'll make it worse. Get back in bed."

"Yeah. That's right."

Parker waited while Kifka got himself back in bed and pulled the sheet up again, and then he turned to the girl and said, "Why'd you let him go out tonight, if he's so sick?"

She looked indignant. "Out! I wouldn't let him go out!"

Kifka was arranging the pillows so he could sit up against them. He stopped and looked at Parker and said, "What's up, Parker? I haven't been out of this bed in three days."

Parker believed it. Kifka wasn't faking sickness, and the girl wasn't faking her answers. He said, "How about your friend makes us some coffee?"

"Tea," Kifka said. "She's got me on tea. You want some?"

Parker shrugged. He didn't care what he drank, just so the girl would leave the room awhile to go get it.

Kifka said, "Janey, be a good girl? Tea all around."

She had come in a few steps from the doorways, and was standing there still holding the sweatshirt in place. She looked more awake now, but also more confused. She said, "He walked in here with a gun, Dan. He's still got it in his hand."

"That's okay, honey, take my word for it. Parker's a friend of mine."

Parker put the gun away in his pocket and showed the girl his empty hand. She said, "What do you take in tea, sugar or lemon?"

He didn't know, so he said, "Neither."

She nodded, turned around, and went out. Because she was pulling the sweatshirt down so hard in front, it was riding very high in back, revealing a bottom as tender as a wheat field.

Kifka laughed, and coughed, and laughed. "Ain't that the

loveliest ass?" he said. "The first time I seen that, in stretch pants, I knew I wanted some. How's the broad you're shacked up with?"

"Dead."

"What?"

Parker went over and shut the bedroom door and leaned his back against it, so the girl wouldn't come in unexpectedly. "I went out tonight for the first time," he said, "to get beer and cigarettes. When I came back, she was dead and the cash was gone."

"The hell you say!"

"There were crossed swords on the wall. Somebody took one down and stuck it right on through her."

"The hell with her," said Kifka, making an angry dismissing gesture. "What's this about the cash?" He was sitting bolt upright in the bed now.

"Gone," Parker told him. "The guy killed her, took the cash, hid out somewhere nearby, waited till he saw me going back in, and called the cops."

"You got out before the cops showed?"

"No. I had to hit heads."

Kifka waved a hand back and forth just above the sheet, like a man dusting a pedestal. "I don't like this," he said. "I don't like this one goddam bit."

"It had to be somebody in on the job," Parker told him. "Who else would know about the money?"

Kifka said, "And you figured me? I look like the guy?" He was all set to be insulted.

Parker said, "You're the only one I know how to find. So I came to talk to you."

"With a gun in your hand?"

"You were supposed to be working. I stopped by the garage and they said you hadn't been around at all. *You* read it, Dan."

Grudgingly, Kifka said, "All right. It was a possibility. But you see the way I am. I started getting this right after the job, right while I was stashing the first car."

"Somebody got the cash," Parker reminded him. He didn't feel like a talk about Kifka's symptoms right now.

Kifka nodded. "So what do we do now?" he said.

The girl was at the door, kicking it with a bare foot. Parker said to Kifka, "Give her a reason to stay out of here."

"Will do."

Parker opened the door and the girl came in carrying a cookie tray with a teapot on it, three cups, a sugar bowl, a little round dish bearing a lemon, and a sharp knife. She put everything down on the table beside the bed. She'd found an apron, pink and white, to supplement the sweatshirt, but it only covered her in front, and when she bent to set the tray down on the table she aimed at Parker again that part that had won Dan Kifka.

Kifka said to her, "Janey honey, Parker and I got to talk awhile, private. Boy talk." Seeing him talking cute to the girl was like watching Smokey the Bear.

The girl turned and looked at Parker. It was obvious she'd decided she didn't like him and never would. She said, "Dan needs his rest."

Parker told her, "He'll get more rest with me than you."

"Just for a few minutes, honey," Kifka said. He could have crumpled her, one-handed, like an empty cigarette package, but instead he put on apologetic look on his face and asked pretty.

Parker waited because that was all he could do, but he didn't like it.

Still, it didn't take as long as he'd expected. The girl pouted a little, and hesitated, and twitched her exposed tail, and made a few more remarks about the state of Kifka's health, and insisted on pouring the tea, but then she gave in and left the room, and closed the door behind her.

Kifka pointed at the closed door. "That's the medicine, boy," he said. "That little girl can keep me as warm as toast."

"The cash," Parker said.

"I know, I know. I'm trying not to think about it."

"That's bright."

"Okay, Parker, don't get feisty. Somebody stole the dough. Look at me, what can I do?"

"You know where a couple of the others are holed up."

Kifka nodded. "Sure I do. Arnie and Little Bob. You want me to contact them?"

"No. I want their addresses. I want to go see if they're still there."

"You think it's one of them? Neither of those guys would pull anything like that, Parker; I've known them both for years."

Parker said, "Who, then? Clinger?"

"Naw. Who, Clinger? He ain't the type."

"How about Shelly? Or Rudd?"

Kifka shook his head to both of them. "You know those guys as well as I do," he said.

"Somebody took the cash," Parker reminded him. "There's only seven of us. It wasn't me and it isn't you. So that leaves five."

Kifka frowned hard, rumpling his face up like a beagle. "I just can't see it," he said. "It couldn't be some outsider?"

"Sure. Coincidence. I don't mind coincidence, it won't be the first time. A flat worker just happened to pick that apartment while I was out. He didn't know Ellie was there, and she saw him and he figured she could identify him, so he took the sword down off the wall and killed her. Then he found the cash by accident and took off. Except burglars don't like to kill if they can avoid it; they'd rather run. And why should he blow the whistle to the cops after I go back in the apartment?"

Kifka nodded reluctantly. "Yeah, it don't sound probable," he admitted.

"Maybe it was a stranger after all," Parker told him. "I'll believe it after I've checked and found out for sure it wasn't any one of us."

"That makes sense, I guess."

Parker looked around. "You got pencil and paper?"

24

"Ask Janey. There ought to be some out in the living room."

Parker went over and opened the door and looked out. Janey was sitting in a basket chair across the room reading a paperback. Parker said, "We need pencil and paper. Just one sheet of paper."

She got to her feet without a word, dropped the book on the chair, and walked across the room to where a secretary stood in the corner. She opened it and started looking for a pencil. She was still dressed the same way, and she'd been sitting in a cane chair, and her bottom now looked like a rounded pink waffle.

She came over finally with ballpoint pen and a small notepad. "Is it going to be much longer?"

Parker took pen and pad from her. "A minute or two." He shut the door in her face and went back to the bed. "You want to give me the addresses?"

"They're together," Kifka told him. "Arnie and Little Bob, the both of them. They're at a place called Vimorama, out on route 12N, about two miles out of town."

"Vimorama." Parker wrote it down.

"It's a health-food place," Kifka told him. "They got all kinds of carrot juice there, crap like that. And like cabins in back. In the summertime they run like a diet farm there; fat people go out and spend a week and don't eat nothing but the carrot juice."

"They're in one of the cabins?"

"Yeah. Number four. You know how to get to 12N?"

"No."

"You know Ridgeworth Boulevard, that's where the hotel is where you stayed when you first came to town."

Parker nodded.

"Well, you take that out past the hotel, going so the hotel is on your right, and you just stay on it out of town and it turns into 12N. Vimorama's about two miles beyond the city limits, on the right. There's a City Line Diner on your left, and you go just about two miles past that."

Parker said, "All right. You got a phone number here?"

"VIctor 6-2598."

Parker wrote it down and said, "I'll get in touch with you, let you know what the story is."

"Good."

Parker got to his feet and started for the door, but Kifka said, "How much was it?"

Parker turned. "What?"

"You counted it, didn't you? The take? How much was it?"

"A hundred thirty-four thousand."

"I get a seventh," Kifka said. "How much is that?"

"About nineteen grand."

"Nineteen grand." Kifka savored the words on his tongue. "I could use nineteen grand," he said.

"So could I."

Kifka nodded. "Sure. You want your seventh, too."

"That's right." Parker turned away again, opened the door, and went into the living room. He said to Janey, "He's yours again."

She immediately dropped the book and got to her feet. "Good."

Kifka was never going to get healthy with Janey around. But then, maybe he didn't care. Parker went on out and shut the apartment door.

He went downstairs and outside and started down the exterior steps to the sidewalk when a voice shouted from across the street, "Hey!" and then there was the sound of a shot.

Parker dove the last four steps, rolled across the sidewalk, and came up against a parked car. A second shot sounded, and the side window of the car shattered, raining glass down on him.

Parker got to hands and knees and crawled hurriedly around the rear of the car. Across the way there was a narrow blacktop driveway hemmed in on both sides by the sheer walls of apartment buildings. With the third shot, Parker saw a muzzle flash in the darkness within that driveway. He dragged a gun out of his topcoat pocket, braced his arm on the bumper of the car, and fired at the muzzle flash.

Footsteps clattered, receding, somebody running away along the blacktop.

Parker ran over that way, flattened himself against a wall, and edged slowly around the corner till he could see into the driveway. At the far end the driveway split, going to left and right behind the apartment buildings. There was a wall at the far end, with a light attached to it. There was no one moving in the alley between Parker and the light. Whoever he was, he'd already made the turn, one way or the other, and was gone. Even the sound of his running footsteps was now gone.

But he'd left something behind, a bulky bundle lying against one of the side walls.

Parker approached it cautiously, but it didn't move. He bent and rolled it over. It was a man. It was the clown in the mackinaw, the follower, the one who wanted his thirty-seven dollars from Dan Kifka.

He'd been shot in the side of the head by a gun of too large a caliber for the job. Kifka now owed thirty-seven dollars to the clown's estate.

It had been the clown who had shouted. The voice had rung with familiarity, but at the time Parker hadn't been concerned with wondering who it was. Now he thought back and remembered it, and it had been the voice of the clown here.

None of it made sense. The clown had been alone before, and had obviously had nothing to do with anything but his own thirty-seven bucks. But now he'd been here with somebody else, and he'd obviously been involved in a lot more than thirty-seven dollars.

Parker's shot hadn't killed him. He'd been shot from close range, not from across the street.

The way it looked, the two of them had been waiting here for Parker to come out. When he did, the second man was going to kill him. But the clown here shouted a warning, and the second man shot him instead and then tried to get Parker anyway and missed.

That told *what* happened, by an educated guess, but not *why*.

27

Why was the clown here? Why did he shout? Why was he killed? And who was the second man?

Maybe it was an outsider after all. There was too much that made no sense; maybe it would start making sense if the guy who now had the cash wasn't one of the seven who'd worked the heist after all.

One thing was sure. This changed the plans.

Parker recrossed the street and went back upstairs to Kifka's apartment and knocked on he door. When the girl opened it this time she was wearing just the sweatshirt again and she looked a little flushed. Also irritated.

Parker went in and shut the door. "Tell Dan I'm sleeping on the sofa," he said. "If you heard the shots out there, that's why. I'll talk to Dan again in the morning."

She said, "Sure you don't want to come in and watch?"

"I already know how."

Parker sat down on the sofa and ignored her. He hadn't bothered to take his topcoat off yet because he was thinking. If the hijacker wasn't one of the original group, then where did he connect? There had only been seven of them in on the operation from the beginning, on equal shares . . . .

4

The job had been set up within the last month. Parker had come north on the run, leaving years of careful work in ruins behind him. He'd needed a fresh stake, and when a slot in this operation was offered him he'd grabbed at it.

Parker was a heister by profession, an institutional robber who stole from banks or jewelry stores or armored cars. He worked only as a member of a team, never as a single-o, and he'd been at this profession nineteen years. For most of that time he'd had a false name and a cover identity within which he lived while spending the profits of his work and out of which he moved once or twice a year to replenish the kitty. But all of that had gone to hell now. As a result of trouble on a piece of work over a year ago his fingerprints had gone on file with the law for the first time, and more trouble just two months ago had connected those fingerprints with the cover identity. Parker had had to leave fast, abandoning bank accounts, abandoning a way of life, everything.

When he'd come north at the wheel of a stolen car, with less than a hundred bills to his name, he'd contacted a few of the men he'd worked with in the past, letting it be known he was available for any job in the offing. He'd holed up in a place outside Scranton called the Green Glen Motel, run by an old hooker named Madge, and a week later a telephone call had come from Dan Kifka.

It was a strange conversation. In the first place, neither of them wanted to say anything specific over a machine as public

29

and leaky as a telephone and in the second place, Kifka didn't really believe he was talking to Parker.

He referred to that immediately after identifying himself, saying, "This is a new number for you, isn't it?"

Parker knew what he meant. In the past no one had ever been able to contact him direct. Anyone who wanted to talk to Parker about business had to send a message through a guy named Joe Sheer, a retired jugger living outside Omaha. But Joe was dead now, a part of the trouble that had cost Parker everything but his neck.

He said, "I just moved. You hear about Joe?"

"Hear what?"

"He died. I went to the funeral."

"Oh. I tried calling you there, but no answer."

"That's why."

Kifka hesitated, and then said, "Well, I just called to say hello, see how things are going. You working?"

"Looking for an opening," Parker told him.

"Good luck."

"Thanks."

"If you see Little Bob Negli out your way, tell him hello for me."

"I will," Parker said, knowing Kifka meant he wouldn't be coming out to Scranton himself but would be sending Little Bob. He said, "He knows about my face, doesn't he?" He'd had plastic surgery done last year, and hadn't met up with Little Bob since then.

"He knows," Kifka said.

Little Bob came out two nights later. Parker was lying fully clothed on the bed in his motel unit, watching television with the sound off, when the knock came at the door. He got to his feet, switched on the light and off the television set, and unlocked the door.

It was Madge, who owned the place. In her sixties now, she was one of the few hookers in the history of the world who really did save her money. When age retired her she'd bought this motel, it being the closest she could get legitimately to her old profession. She was too talkative and too nervous to be a madam, but she could run a motel where the rooms were rented mostly by the hour. She could also be trusted, so people in Parker's line of work occasionally used her place for meetings or cooling off.

She came in now and shut the door, saying, "Little Bob Negli's here. You want to talk to him?" She was still bone-thin, which once had been her main selling point. Her white hair was harsh-looking and brittle, chopped short in an Italian cut. Curved black lines had been drawn on her face where the eyebrows had been plucked, and her long curving fingernails were painted scarlet, but she wore no lipstick; her mouth was a pale scar in a thin, deeply lined face.

She always dressed young, in bright sweaters and stretch pants, with dangling Navaho earrings and jangling charm bracelets. Inside the young clothing was an old body, but inside the old body was a young woman. Madge would hold onto 1920 until the day she died; she'd never had a better year and wasn't likely to.

Now she said, "Little Bob's in my room behind the office. You want to go there, or have him come here, or what?"

"I'll go there."

"I'll fix drinks," she said.

Parker didn't want drinks, but he said nothing. Madge had to turn everything into a party. Every day was old home week.

They left Parker's room and walked down the sidewalk in front of the units toward the office. "It's good to have the old bunch around," Madge was saying, and told him who'd been here last month, and two months ago, and six months ago. This was the one thing Parker couldn't take about her, her gossiping. She never opened her mouth to the wrong people, but she never shut it with insiders. Parker walked along beside her now and let her chatter wash off him like rain.

They went into the office, where Ethel was sitting at the desk. Ethel was about twenty-five, mentally retarded, Madge's cleaning girl and general assistant. Madge told her, "I'll be in back with the boys," and she nodded without saying anything.

31

Little Bob Negli was sitting on the green leatherette sofa in the back room, smoking a cigar half as tall as him. He was a shrimp: four feet eleven and one-half inches tall. He had the little man's cockiness, standing and moving like the bantam-weight champion of the world, chomping dollar cigars, wearing clothes as fancy as he could find, sporting a pompadour in his black hair that damn near brought his height up to normal. He looked like something that had been shrunk and preserved in the nineteenth century.

He got to his feet when Madge and Parker walked in and frowned up at Parker as though he had a really tough decision to make and the civilized world hung on his answer. He said to Madge, "That's really Parker?"

"It really is," she said. "He traded one sour puss for another. Wait'll you spend five minutes with him, you'll see. He hasn't changed a bit, still the same old Cheery Charlie, life of the party."

Parker said, "Maybe Bob wants to talk business."

Madge grinned. "See what I mean? What do you want to drink, Parker?"

"Nothing."

"Maybe that's your trouble. Bob, you want a refill, just holler."

"Will do, Madge."

She went out, and Negli said, "I wouldn't call it an improvement exactly."

"That's enough about the face," Parker told him. He pulled a foam-rubber chair over in front of the sofa and sat down.

Negli stayed on his feet a few seconds longer. He seemed to be trying to make up his mind about something, maybe whether he should be insulted or not. But then he sat down and said, "Business, then. You interested in a score?"

"That depends."

"On what?"

"The take, the risk, and who I'm supposed to be working with."

"Of course. That's to be expected. But if the take is good

and the risk is low and the people are known to you, you're interested?"

Parker nodded.

"All right." Negli put the long cigar in his mouth and talked around it. "The take," he said, "is between a hundred and a hundred fifty G. The risk is practically nil. The people, so far, are Dan Kifka and Arnie Feccio and me."

"So far," Parker echoed. "How many you figure all told?"

"The details aren't all worked out yet. We figure six or seven."

"That's a big string."

Negli shrugged. "We want risk low, we got to have enough men."

"That's fifteen to twenty G a man, depending on how much and how many."

"Sure. Figure fifteen minimum."

"What's the job?"

"Gate receipts. College football gate receipts."

Parker frowned. "How do you figure low risk?"

"It all depends on the plan. We've already got a way in, and we ought to be able to make some kind of advantage out of the traffic jam after the game. There's always a traffic jam after a football game."

"All you've got," Parker said, "is a way in and an itch."

"You ever hear a job start with more?"

"It better have more before it's worked."

"So come in and see Dan; you know where he lives. He'll give you everything we got."

"Anybody asking ace shares?"

"No. Equal divvy, share and share alike."

Parker considered, and then nodded. "I'll come in and talk," he said. "I don't promise any more than that."

"Of course not." Negli got to his feet, the cigar at a jaunty angle in the corner of his mouth. "You'll like this operation," he said. "It's neat and clean. And profitable."

They left the room, and out in the office Madge said, "Done so soon? Stick around, we'll talk, it's a slow night."

"Got to be going, Madge," Negli said. "Wish I could stay, but that's how it is." To Parker he said, "Tomorrow night, nine o'clock."

"I'll be there."

Madge started talking again, urging them to stay and chat. Parker assumed she was talking to Negli instead of him, and went straight back to his room. He switched the television on without the sound, left the room lights off, and lay on the bed to watch and think.

Sometimes there was an advantage in doing a job in the middle of a crowd, and if Negli and Kifka actually did have a way into this stadium, there was no reason why they couldn't figure a way out again. It all depended on the details.

The next night, at nine, he was in Kifka's apartment. There was no cheerleader there that time. Instead, there was Little Bob Negli and Arnie Feccio. Feccio was a florid moustachioed type with a beer-barrel torso and oily black hair. He looked more Greek than Italian, and whichever nationality he looked he had to be a restaurant owner. He'd tried to substantiate his looks a few times, but his restaurants always went broke and he always had to go back to his regular profession to get himself out of debt.

The four of them sat around a table in Kifka's living room, and Kifka, with the help of maps and diagrams, told Parker what they had:

"It's Monequois Stadium, just outside town on Western Avenue. Monequois's one of them hoity-toity Ivy League colleges, nothing but money, and this is their new stadium. Saturday, the sixteenth of November, is their big game against Plainfield, the big deal for the whole season. And the nice thing, it's what they call inter-conference—it don't count in their regular season, they play in different conferences."

Parker said, "What makes that nice?"

"The gate receipts are different," Kifka told him. "It ain't a regular season game, so the gate receipts go to some charity or fund or something, and season tickets don't count. Also, no mail orders, no advance sales at all. It's a big deal, see what I mean? Like the World Series. The box office opens at six in the morning the day of the game, and there's always these clowns that stay up all night to buy the first tickets."

Little Bob Negli said, "You see the beauty, Parker? Except for student tickets, student passes, whatever they call them, every seat in the house is paid for cash on the barrelhead the day of the game. And all that cash has to be right there in the stadium when the game starts."

Parker nodded. "So it's a big score," he said. "If we can get at it."

"We can get at it." Kifka spread out a diagram on the table, facing so Parker could see it best. "This is the stadium. They got three box offices where they sell tickets, North Gate, East Gate, and South Gate. These squares here with the X's in them. About once an hour the cash is collected and brought around to the stadium building here at the west end of the stadium. All your offices and locker rooms and everything are in this building. Now, your finance office is on the second floor, and that's where the money's delivered."

Parker said, "How?"

"Armed guards in pairs. They walk it along a corridor under the stands. They wouldn't be that tough to hit, but they never carry more than a couple grand at a time anyway."

Parker nodded.

"Now," Kifka said, "in the finance office the cash is counted and stacked and banded and put in money boxes to go to the bank. They get it done by the time the last quarter is starting so the armored car can get out of there before the traffic jam starts. The armored car doesn't come till they phone for it, so it isn't there very long, just long enough to fill up and take off. It's bracketed by municipal police in riot cars all the way to the bank. The bank has a special deal where it has people down there even though it's Saturday, and the money goes in and gets checked all over again right away."

Parker said, "What sort of guard in the finance office?"

"You got four armed men in there, private police, plus six employees. The way in, you pass through a locked guarded door into a corridor and along the corridor is the finance office. You knock there and they check you with a peephole before they open up."

Parker nodded. "What about the size of it? It's going to be mostly small bills."

Arnie Feccio answered, saying, "We figure two big suitcases ought to do it."

"That's a lot of weight."

Negli smiled and said, "We don't want to have to run with it anyway, Parker."

Parker said, "We'll see." To Kifka he said, "I understand you've got a way in."

"A beauty," Kifka told him. "A natural."

"Let's hear it."

"We go in on Friday." He stopped and grinned at Parker, waiting for Parker to do cartwheels. When Parker just sat there and looked at him, Kifka belatedly went on with it: "We go in Friday afternoon," he said. "We get into the finance office then and we spend the night there. Saturday we collar every employee the minute he walks through the door. We're on top of the situation from the beginning. The cash is brought in; we have the employees stow it right in our suitcases."

Feccio said, "What do you think, Parker?"

"I don't know yet. How do you get in?"

"At the entrances," Kifka told him, "they got these ornamental gates, you know? With the spear points on top and all that jazz. So they don't quite reach to the top of the entranceway. I can get Bob up high enough, and he can squeeze through."

"Like an eel," said Negli. He demonstrated by wriggling his hand through the air.

"There's doors here and there in the wall," said Kifka, "besides the gates themselves. They're kept locked, but you can unlock them easy from inside."

"What if somebody sees you and Bob at the gate?"

Kifka grinned. "Early birds. First ones on line at the North Gate. We got this all worked out, Parker, believe me. The

South Gate is where the newspaper photographers always take the pictures of the nuts, and the East Gate is right on the main drag, so we do it around at the North Gate. Monequois Park is across the road there, and if anybody drives by what are they going to see?"

"All right. Then what?"

"We got three locks to get through and we're in the finance office. Then we wait till morning."

Negli said, "It's good, Parker, you know it is. It's worth your time coming here."

"If it plays like Dan says it does, and if there's a way out."

Kifka said, "So what do you want to do?"

"Is there anything doing out to the stadium tonight or tomorrow morning?"

"Middle of the week? Nothing."

"Then we do a run-through," Parker said. "Tonight. We want lock impressions anyway, so we can move faster when the time comes."

"Good idea."

They ran it through later that night, and it worked just as Kifka had said it would. Negli went over the North Gate and a minute later let the other three through a green door in the brick wall about ten paces away to the left. They were under the grandstand in a kind of concrete tunnel. Lighting their way with flashlights, they followed the tunnel around to the right and came out in the basement of the stadium building, next to a metal staircase. They went up two flights and Arnie Feccio worked silently and speedily on a locked door. There was no alarm system here, and no guards inside the stadium at night, although private police did patrol the general area by car.

Kifka led the way past the first locked door to the second, which led onto the corridor to the finance office. Feccio got them through this door, too, and then through the third, and they were in the finance office.

The finance office was actually three offices separated by room dividers of wood and glass, plus a small closed-off workroom containing supplies and a mimeograph machine.

They looked the place over, decided the workroom would be the place to spend the night when the time came, and retraced their steps, Feccio taking the time to study the locks as they went so they'd have keys when they came back.

Outside in the car, Kifka said, "Well? How does it look?"

"We can get in," Parker said.

Kifka nodded. "Right. And the question is, can we get out? Right?"

"That's right."

"If we can get in, we can get out. We'll have to work on it."

"Tomorrow," Parker said. "It's been a long day. I need a place to stay while I'm here."

"With a woman or without?"

Parker hesitated, then said, "With." Not that he expected to want her, not just yet. Before a job he never had any interest in women, or in anything else but the job itself. But he would want her afterward, when he would make up for lost time.

Kifka had gotten him Ellie. Not exactly a pro, hardly an amateur. She wasn't sharing her place with anybody at the moment and she didn't mind sharing with Parker so long as he came with an introduction from somebody she knew and was willing to pay for the groceries and incidentals. She seemed surprised when Parker let her know the first night that nothing was expected just yet, but she didn't seem to care one way or the other.

That almost summed her up. In her clothing, her appearance, her apartment, her life, in everything, she didn't care one way or the other. She was a good-looking girl, but Parker never really noticed it unless she was nude. She wore her clothing so sloppily that with it on she looked like a lesbian gym teacher on a cross-country hike. Her black hair was too long and too full and too infrequently combed. She daubed lipstick on from time to time, but otherwise she never used makeup. And she treated the apartment the same way she treated herself: negligently.

She had some sort of daytime job that didn't require she be particularly neat. Parker never asked her what her work was, and she never volunteered the information. Her style was very much like Parker's own, silent and self-contained. They spent hours in the same room without either saying a word.

Parker was pleased by her. She didn't jabber away at him, and he never had to tell her anything twice. Kifka had done better than could have been expected.

The job pleased him too. In more sessions with the others, they gradually worked out a plan for getting themselves and the cash out of the stadium and safely in the clear. The final plan needed seven men, so they recruited three more, all pros they'd worked with in the past. Abe Clinger was a fast talker, could be a guard or a finance office employee or whatever you wanted. Ray Shelly and Pete Rudd were drivers and general strongarms.

Kifka was actually running the job, though he wasn't asking more than his seventh. But he arranged for the financing, and he was the one who'd seen the possibilities in the job to begin with, having worked at the stadium the year before. His apartment remained headquarters, where they met and worked out the details.

Financing ran steep. They wanted a minimum of five pistols and two machine guns, plus two cars and an ambulance and a truck. The only things that really caused trouble were the machine guns, unlicensed ownership of which is a Federal offense. But they got everything they needed in plenty of time.

They kept the vehicles in a closed-down gas station on a secondary highway out of town. The two cars were a seven-year-old black Buick, a fat monster that looked like something with gland trouble, and a little gray Renault Dauphine, which looked like something the Buick had just spat out. The truck was a gray GM van, four years old, with a rotten transmission. The ambulance was a smaller version of the van, the sort of ambulance used in wars and on airfields and at football games.

All the vehicles but the Buick needed work of one kind or another. The stunted rear seat of the Renault was pulled out to leave plenty of room for the two suitcases. The van was given a company name on its doors—CITY SCRAP METAL CORP.—and a bunch of old metal barrels were put in the back, lined along one side. Two long two-by-twelve boards were laid in on the floor.

The ambulance was the most work. It had been used as a grocer's delivery truck most recently, so it had to be completely repainted, two coats of white sprayed on and then the red crosses painted in place. Lights that had been removed when it had stopped being an ambulance were put back, and two boards like those in the van were put on the floor in back.

By Friday night they were ready. At nine-thirty all of them but Shelly and Rudd were in the Buick, parked by the North Gate. Kifka and Negli got out carrying folding chairs and brown paper bags full of sandwiches and took up their post by the gate. When the coast was clear, Kifka boosted Negli over the fence, then sat down on his camp chair and unfolded a newspaper to read by the streetlight. A couple of minutes later he folded the paper up again and stretched, which meant Negli had opened the door in the darkness to the right of the gate. Parker and Feccio and Clinger got out of the Buick, Parker carrying the two suitcases, Feccio and Clinger carrying blanket-wrapped parcels that were the machine guns.

The door was open, Negli inside waiting for them. They went through and shut the door and Negli took out a flashlight with electric tape over most of the glass in front, so when he flicked it on only a thin beam of light arrowed out to show them where they were.

Outside, Parker knew, Kifka would wait a few more minutes, then gather up his gear and get into the Buick and drive home. He and Shelly and Rudd wouldn't have anything to do until tomorrow.

Inside, Negli led the way with the flashlight. They'd been over this route before, but this time it was easier because they had keys for all the doors. They settled into the finance office storeroom and waited for morning.

The day started early. Employees and guards dribbled in between seven and eight-thirty, and each was taken care of in turn. The guards were stripped of their uniforms, tied and gagged, and left in the storeroom with Negli holding one of the machine guns on them. With any operation of this kind, a machine gun's main use was psychological. Nobody wanted to have to fire one of them, because of the mess and the racket they made. But merely showing a machine gun to a mark was usually enough to make him a lot more peaceful and agreeable than any other weapon could have.

After all the employees had arrived, the money started coming in. Feccio stood out of sight of the corridor door, holding the second machine gun on the employees seated at their tables. He and Parker, who answered the door every time more money arrived, were now dressed in guard uniforms. Clinger, now in shirt sleeves, played the part of an employee, accepting and signing for each delivery of money as it came in.

They had the employees stack the cash in the suitcases without counting it. The sacks of change that also came in were ignored, being too bulky and awkward for their value, as well as being almost impossible to spend.

Parker looked at his watch at eleven o'clock and knew the others were getting started on the outside. Rudd was getting the truck and driving it to a place seven blocks from the stadium, inside the city limits. Shelly by now had driven the Renault inside the ambulance, where it fit snugly but did fit, and he was ready to leave for the stadium when the time came. And Kifka was driving the Buick to meet Rudd, to leave the Buick parked against the curb directly behind the truck, so that space would be sure to be available when it was needed.

The football game began at one-thirty, and the box offices closed at one-fifty. By five after two, as the second quarter was starting with Monequois ahead seven to three and Shelly was starting the ambulance engine and heading toward the stadium, the employees in the finance office were stacking the last of the gate receipts into the two suitcases. Parker checked with Negli, but the guards were still being good.

Two-fifteen. Monequois was ahead now ten to three, and Shelly was arriving in the ambulance at the stadium's East Gate, where the patrolman waved him on through. Shelly, aseptic in white jacket and white shirt and white trousers, waved back and drove on into the stadium. A short cinder driveway led him around the corner of the end zone bleachers and out into the view of seventy-four thousand people.

As with most such stadiums, this one had been built for more sports than football. A cinder track made a huge oval around the football field, for track events. Shelly drove slowly along this the length of the field, on the south side, and headed for the stadium building at the far end. On his left, thousands of people cheered and hollered and jumped up and down. On his right, Plainfield was finally on the march. Shelly felt a little self-conscious, but nobody was actually looking at him. There's always an ambulance or two along the sidelines at a football game, but the fans don't like to look at it or be reminded it's there.

One hundred yards, still and all, had never been so long. Shelly honked for a girl cheerleader toting a huge megaphone to get the hell out of the way. She got, glaring at him. He passed a legitimate ambulance parked on the grass between the cinder track and the western end zone; the driver, lounging against the front fender, turned his head and waved languidly. Shelly waved back.

At the western end of the stadium, the cinder path ended and Shelly crossed a narrow patch of grass to a lane of blue-gray stones that led around to a blacktop parking area behind the building. Shelly drove around there and parked against the rear wall.

The parking lot was full of the cars of employees of the stadium and a few chartered buses from Plainfield. There was no one in sight; bus drivers and all, they were around on the other side of the building watching the game.

Upstairs, Parker went over to the window and looked out and saw Shelly down there. He motioned to him and turned back to help with the finishing up. The employees had to be tied and gagged like the guards and dragged into the store-room. When that was done, Parker took the rope he'd brought in with him, tied one end to the radiator, and attached the other end to the two suitcases. Feccio helped him lower the two suitcases down to Shelly, who took them off the rope and stowed them away in the back of the Renault inside the ambulance. They lowered the machine guns next, and finally they came down the rope themselves, one at a time. Parker and Clinger crawled into the back of the ambulance and squeezed into the Renault. Feccio, still in his guard uniform, sat up front with Shelly in the cab of the ambulance, while Negli found enough room between the back of the Renault and the rear doors of the ambulance to be more or less comfortable.

It was now two twenty-five. Plainfield was on the Monequois eight-yard line, first and goal to go, three minutes and seventeen seconds left in the first half. Monequois was still leading ten to three. Plainfield had one chance to tie the score before the half. The seventy-four thousand fans present had never seen a more exciting ball game.

So it was just an added fillip when the ambulance came tearing around from behind the stadium building, red lights flashing and siren screaming, racing across the cinder track from one end of the field to the other while the Plainfield quarterback threw an incompleted pass into the end zone and cheerleaders scattered in all directions. The ambulance roared out through the East Gate, turned right, and shrieked away toward the city.

It went one block, and the siren stopped and the red lights clicked off.

Another block and the ambulance pulled to the curb. Feccio jumped out, ran around back, opened the rear doors, and helped Negli position the boards for Parker to back the Renault out. They were on a side street with no traffic and no pedestrians, but they didn't care if they were seen or not. Neither of these vehicles mattered.

Feccio and Negli got back into the rear of the ambulance, shutting the doors after them. Shelly kicked the ambulance into motion again, turned left at the next corner, left again at the next, and drove for five minutes at high speed, rapidly leaving the city behind. He stopped at a roadside ice-cream stand, closed for the season, behind which Feccio and Negli had stashed their car. They abandoned the ambulance there, and Feccio and Negli drove Shelly to his hideout and then went on to theirs.

Behind them, Parker and Clinger had gone off in the opposite direction in the Renault. Clinger looked at his watch and said, "Two-thirty on the button."

Parker said, "Good."

He turned a corner, and three blocks ahead on the right was the truck. As he approached it, the Buick pulled out from behind it and stopped in the middle of the street. Kifka got out and ran around to the back of the van, where Rudd was already placing the boards.

Parker angled the Renault in behind the Buick and stopped long enough for Kifka and Rudd to be sure the boards were positioned right, and then he drove the Renault up inside the truck.

No one saw it happen. A factory, closed on Saturday, was on their right, and the high board fence of a junkyard was on the left.

Parker and Clinger got out of the Renault while Kifka and Rudd were shoving the boards back up into the truck. The four of them all worked inside the truck for a minute, moving the empty barrels into position across the opening at the rear of the truck, lashing them into place with ropes. Their unused pistols were tossed into the back of the Renault with the machine guns and the suitcases.

"We didn't need all this extra," Clinger said as they were putting the barrels in place. "They still don't know what happened back there."

"You couldn't count on it ahead of time," Kifka told him. "If the alarm went out right away, they'd know nothing but an ambulance had left the stadium recently, and they'd be all over the place looking for that ambulance. We had to be able to make a fast switch to another car, and then we had to be able to hide that car and the loot. That's where baby came in." He

44

motioned at the Renault. "It's like a traveling briefcase. Out of the ambulance, into the truck."

"All the same," Clinger said, "I'm just as happy we didn't need all this."

They got down out of the truck, and Parker put the last barrel in position. Then he crawled through the glassless window at the front of the box into the cab. Kifka and Rudd and Clinger got into the Buick and took off.

Now, for the next five days, the money was Parker's responsibility. He knew where Kifka was staying because Kifka was staying at home. He didn't know where any of the others were staying because there was no need for him to know; it wouldn't be bright to contact them anyway, and at the time it didn't seem there'd be any reason to contact them. In five days they would all get together again, this time at Ellie's place, and divvy up the money. By splitting up this way and by not trying to clear out of the city and the area, they would make it more difficult for the law to get any kind of lead to them.

Parker just sat in the truck and smoked and waited. A little after three, police cars started rushing by, hurrying this way and that, and Parker heard sirens sounding in the distance, but nobody stopped to question him or search the truck. One prowl car did slow down, but a truck full of metal barrels could hardly be involved in the robbery.

At four o'clock, Parker started the engine and drove slowly away from there. He drove all the way through the city to the freight yards and parked the truck on Railroad Street, down from the main freight office. Parked and laden trucks lined both sides of the street along here, most of them here for the weekend. Parker climbed out, left the truck doors unlocked, and walked away. He walked three blocks, caught a cab, and went on back to the apartment. Ellie wasn't home; he found out later she'd gone to the game. She was a Monequois fan.

At nine that night he went back downtown and picked up the truck and drove it over to the block containing Ellie's apartment building. Going through the window between body and cab each time, he transferred everything from the Renault to the closet of Ellie's apartment. The suitcases he carried up in one trip, and then the machine guns wrapped in blankets. The pistols he carried up in his pockets. When everything was stashed, he drove the truck downtown again, abandoned it for the last time, took another cab back, and went in to see Ellie. The job was done; he could feel himself unwinding.

Seeing how lackadaisical Ellie was about everything else in life, Parker hadn't expected her to be more in bed than a receptacle, but she surprised him. He had found the one thing that made her pay attention. For three days and nights they hardly left the bed at all, and the whole time she was nothing but stifled mumblings and hard-muscled legs and hot breath and demanding arms and a sweat-slick pulsing belly. All the passion that had been dammed up inside Parker while his one-track mind had been concentrating on the robbery now burst forth in one long sustained silent explosion, and Ellie absorbed it all the way a soundproof room absorbs a shout.

By the third night the pace had begun to slacken, and waking up from one of his intermittent naps Parker felt the need for fresh air and a quiet walk. They were out of cigarettes and they would need beer soon after breakfast or whatever meal this was Ellie promised to make him, so he got dressed and went out, and he was gone ten minutes.

It was a fast ten minutes, and the time since then had been fast too. Ellie was dead, the suitcases were gone. Parker had had a brawl with a couple of cops and he'd been trailed by a thirty-seven-dollar moocher and he'd been shot at by person or persons unknown who hadn't killed him but who had killed the moocher as a consolation prize.

It was time to start pushing back.

PART TWO

1

Parker looked at the pistols scattered all over the kitchen table. He'd taken them out of all his pockets to decide which ones he wanted to carry.

There were four of them: a Colt Cobra .38 Special revolver with the two-inch barrel and a hammer shroud to keep it from snagging in a pocket, a Smith & Wesson Terrier .32, also with a two-inch barrel, a Colt Super Auto .38 automatic, and an Astra Firecat .25 automatic. It was the Terrier he'd fired last night; all the others still carried full loads.

Four guns was twice as many as he needed. He chose the two Colts, checked them to be sure they were full, and carried them over to where his topcoat was draped over a chair. He put the guns in the pockets, then carried the other two into the bedroom.

Dan was no different this morning, no better and no worse. From the night he'd obviously had with Janey, just holding his own was already a medical miracle. He looked up from the tea Janey made him drink between bouts, and said, "You ready to talk now?" He had practically no voice at all this morning.

Parker said, "You heeled?"

"Not so's you'd notice."

"You better be. You want these two? This one's been fired once."

Kifka shrugged. "Why not? Stick 'em under the pillow."

Janey said, "Keep them out of the bed. Put them on the night table if you have to."

Parker looked from her to Kifka. Kifka shrugged again, and

Parker put the guns on the night table. Then he said, "How much does she know?"

"Enough."

"About the operation?"

Kifka nodded. "My part in it, and what it was. And about Ellie being killed."

Parker dragged a chair over closer to the bed and sat down. He told Kifka about the ambush last night, and about the dead clown. Two police cars and an ambulance had been around the block with screaming sirens last night, about half an hour after Parker had gone back upstairs, so the clown was long gone. Parker said, "You can figure cops knocking on the door today, routine questions, did you hear anything, see anything."

Kifka said, "Janey can take care of it."

"I better get dressed," she said. She was still in the sweatshirt, or in it again.

Kifka told her, "Stick around." To Parker he said, "I think I know the clown. Morey, his name was. A real loser."

"Any connection with Ellie?"

"Naw, not Morey. He was mucho married."

"Did he know her?"

Kifka shook his head. "Different circles, man. Morey I knew from work, Ellie I knew from play." He grinned and winked at Janey, who said, "Big man."

Parker told him, "If Negli or Feccio or any of the others had done it, he would of handled the whole thing different. He wouldn't of killed Ellie unless he absolutely had to, and then he wouldn't of used that stupid sword. He might of tried to tie me up with the law, but just to give himself extra time to clear out. He wouldn't of hung around to take potshots. If one of the boys had the cash now, he'd either be playing it cool and quiet right where he's supposed to be hiding out anyway, ready to get all surprised when he hears how the dough's gone, or he'd be in Arizona or someplace by now."

Kifka nodded. "I know. It rings like an amateur."

"There's two possibilities," Parker told him. "First, one of us in the job talked too much, and somebody he talked to decided to go after the dough. Second, it was sombody who went there to kill Ellie for the main bit and he just stumbled across the money and figured why not."

Kifka said, "I think it's got to be number two. We've all been around long enough to keep our mouths shut."

"Maybe."

"Like Janey," Kifka said. "You don't have to wonder about her. She didn't know your girl, and she didn't know where the dough was stashed. All she knew about was my part, and you probably told Ellie just as much."

Parker hadn't, but he let it ride. He shrugged.

Kifka put his teacup down and said, "What we want to do now, we want to get everybody together, we want to get some manpower on this thing. We got to get our dough back."

"Can we use this place?"

Janey said, "Dan, you're sick."

Parker told her, "Here's his chance to get healthy," and she looked insulted.

Kifka said, "Sure we use this place. What other place do we have?"

"All right." Parker got to his feet. "I'll go get Negli and Feccio. They'll know where some of the others are. You got a car I can use?"

"The Buick's still clean. The keys ought to be over on the dresser there."

Parker went over and found the keys. "I'll be back as soon as I can," he said. "You want to get the hardware out of sight, in case the cops show."

Kifka nodded. He said, "All I can see is those two suitcases in the trunk of some car on its way to the Panama Canal."

"The guy's hanging around," Parker said. "He's an amateur, he lives in this town, he's hanging around."

Kifka said, "Let's hope he doesn't smarten up."

2

The Vimorama was about as pretty as a wax orange and about as lively. Parker let the Buick roll on by and then pulled to the shoulder of the road a hundred feet farther on and switched off the engine. Then he sat there a minute.

Behind him, Vimorama hulked beside the road like a pastel flying saucer. It seemed to be made mostly of orange I-beams and shiny chrome and gleaming glass, with VIMORAMA in huge varicolored letters on the roof and equally huge letters on the sign out by the road. There was no sign of activity either from the main building itself or from the little cabins scattered around behind it like a bunch of colored top hats dropped out of a box.

He was sure he hadn't been followed, but he waited a couple of minutes in the car anyway. When he was positive no one was taking any interest in him he climbed out on the passenger side and walked back down the road to the gravel Vimorama parking lot. He skirted it on the quieter grass and moved swiftly in among the tiny cabins.

Number four was way in back, at the rear of the Vimorama property. Parker rapped on the door and then stood back to give those on the inside a good look at him.

This was a bad moment. It didn't figure the cash had been stolen by an insider, but there was always the chance. If it had been stolen by Negli or Feccio or both, it didn't figure they'd be inside that cabin at all, but there was always the chance. If they'd stolen the money and they were in there anyway, it figured they planned on bluffing it out, but there was always the chance. Parker had been shot at last night and he didn't like setting himself up this way no matter how slim the odds were. He stood tensed, ready to jump.

But all that happened was the door opened and Feccio was standing there in his undershirt and red suspenders. He looked confused. He said, "Parker? What the hell are *you* doing here?"

"Waiting to come in."

"Come, come. Let's not advertise."

Parker went in, and Feccio shut the door behind him.

Unmade twin beds, a metal-cased television set, two metal bureaus, a ceiling light fixture like a serving tray, and linoleum on the floor; the whole thing looked like any cheap motel room or fourth-rate tourist cabin. A little alcove on the right, between the built-in bathroom and the built-in closet, contained shelving holding a twin-burner hot plate and kitchen utensils and cans and boxes of food. A miniature refrigerator nestled under the shelves.

The place was mostly windows, but all of them were thickly covered with dark cloth, like a wartime blackout, so it was night inside the cabin and the ceiling light was on. This place was supposed to be closed for the season; lights from one of the units at night, or any sign of activity through an unshielded window in the daytime, might attract the attention of a passing state trooper.

Negli was sitting in the room's one chair, a foam-rubber and wrought-iron affair. He was as dapper as ever, dressed to the nines, busy unwrapping one of his long cigars. He said, "You know better than this, Parker. It isn't time for us to contact each other. What if you brought the law here?"

"I didn't bring the law."

Negli shrugged. "Still," he said, "this had better be worth it."

Parker studied him sourly. Negli had the little man's courage, the knowledge he could get away with things a bigger man would be called on in a minute. It gave him a nasty disposition, and made Parker itch to tromp him.

Feccio was the other half of the team, the apologizer.

53

"Parker knows what he's doing," he said. "If he's here, he's got a good reason."

"Good enough," Parker said. "I was hijacked. The money's gone."

Feccio just stared. Negli looked up from his cigar, and paused, and said, "Stole it from *you*, Parker?" He said it like he didn't believe it.

Parker went over and picked him up and threw him into the corner. When Negli rolled over with his hand going inside his coat, Parker put his right hand in his topcoat pocket.

Feccio said, "Cut it! Bob, don't you move!"

Negli stayed where he was, half up from the floor, right hand still inside the coat.

Feccio said, "Parker, you know Bob's way. He didn't mean it like it sounded."

Parker said, "Let Negli talk."

Negli said, "I believe you, Parker. You had the dough and you let somebody glom it from you. I believe it."

Feccio walked over in front of Negli and said, "Cut it out, Bob, or I'll take care of you myself."

"The hell, Arnie. What does he want, a medal? We put a lot of work in and he comes around and says he lost the money, somebody took it from him."

"Let's listen to him, what do you say?"

Negli got to his feet, and brushed himself off. "I'll listen to anybody," he said.

Feccio turned to Parker. "We start all over," he said. "You just tell the story and we'll listen."

Parker told them the story. Feccio listened and Negli stood around trying to look insulting. Parker had control of himself now, and he ignored Negli. The little bastard wasn't worth the sweat.

When he was done, Feccio said, "I like the outsider. Somebody wanted your girl dead and he found the cash by accident."

Negli said, "I haven't said word one to anybody outside the group about what we were doing. Neither has Arnie. What about you, talking to the girl? Or Dan and his bimbo?"

Parker shook his head. "Neither one of us told our women anything to worry about."

"Yours knew you had all that cash, didn't she?"

"She never left the apartment from the time I brought the suitcases in. She wasn't out of my sight for three days, not until I went out last night."

Feccio said, "All right, never mind that now. What do you want from us, that's the question."

"If we work together, we can get our cash back."

Feccio nodded. "If we work together," he said, "and if we're lucky. And if the law doesn't get him first."

"They'll be looking for me," Parker said. "They won't think about anybody else when I'm so handy."

Negli said, "That makes you a liability, doesn't it, Parker?"

Before Parker could say anything, Feccio said, "Bob, keep your mouth shut. We don't have time to put up with you now."

Parker said, "Do you know where any of the others are holed up?"

"I know where Shelly is," Feccio said. "I think he knows where to find Clinger and Rudd."

Negli said, "What we ought to do, Arnie, we ought to clear out of here. That dough's gone."

Parker said, "Maybe not."

Negli shook his head. "You're a dreamer. If I had that cash, I'd be a thousand miles from here by now."

"You're a pro. You wouldn't have hung around last night to ambush me."

Feccio said, "This is wasting time. Bob and I'll go talk to Shelly. You want us all to meet someplace?"

"At Dan's. I'll get there as soon as I can."

"Fine."

Parker went to the door, then looked back at Negli. "You don't have to waste time with the rest of us," he said. "You want to take off, go ahead. We'll find something to do with your cut."

Negli made a crooked grin around his cigar. "Forget it,

Parker," he said. "I own a seventh of that pie. As long as there's one chance left at it, I'll stick around."

Parker said, "That's what I thought."

3

BEAUTY SLAIN

SWORD FATAL WEAPON
IN BIZARRE SLAYING

by Robert Hochberg

In one of the most bizarre slayings in city history, police reported last night the discovery of the nude and brutally murdered body of Miss Ellen Marie Canaday, 22, in the bedroom of her apartment at 106-12 Longmans Avenue. Miss Canaday had been fatally stabbed through the chest with an ornamental sword which had been hanging on her apartment wall (photos, page 7).

The suspected slayer, still on the scene when police arrived at the murder apartment, made his escape and is still at large.

Miss Canaday, a model, had lived alone at the Longmans Avenue address about one year. Since the front door had been forced, it is assumed her attacker was not known to her, although police do not discount the possibility of a personal quarrel as a motive in the case.

Detective Lieutenant Albert Murphy, in charge of the investigation, stated the similarities between this slaying and the so-called Strangler murders in the Boston area were too few and minor to imply any necessary connection with those crimes, though Boston police authorities have expressed interest in the investigation of the Canaday case.

Murphy also announced expectation of the early recapture of the man believed to be the slayer (description and artist's rendering of suspect on page 7).

> No comparable slaying has occurred in the local area since 1949,
> when three Norwegian sailors . . . .

Parker stopped reading at that point, scanned down the rest of the story to be sure there wasn't anything else in it he wanted to know, and then switched over to page seven.

The artist's drawing was rotten. It looked just a little like the face Parker used to wear, before he'd had plastic surgery done a year ago, but it didn't look anything like the face he had now.

The written description, in a box beside the bad drawing, was accurate as far as it went, but it didn't go very far. Women and children were obviously eliminated by it, but it still left a hell of a lot of men in the running, all of whom fitted the written description and none of whom—including Parker——looked like the artist's rendering.

In addition to the drawing and description, there were three photographs on the page. One showed Ellie's bedroom, with the body removed. One showed a uniformed cop looking blankly at the sprung front door that Parker had kicked in. And one showed a plainclothes cop holding the sword out in front of himself and looking at it as though he wondered what the hell it was and why he was supposed to be holding it.

Under this last photo was the caption:

> Detective Third Grade William Dougherty studies murder weapon for clues. Sword, taken by slayer from apartment wall, had been wiped clean of all fingerprints.

The way the world usually worked, Detective Lieutenant Albert Murphy, the one who'd been quoted all over the place in the main story about the killing and who was listed as being in charge of the investigation, wouldn't know a damn thing about the murder or the investigation or anything else. The way the world usually worked, it was Detective Third Grade William Dougherty who would really be running the case and would know what was going on.

Parker folded the paper and put it down on the table. He was sitting in a luncheonette downtown, not far from where he'd left the truck four days ago. The noon hour rush would be starting in a little while, but right now the place was almost empty. The walls were beige and the booths were green.

There was an untouched cup of coffee on the table beside the paper. Parker looked at it, shook his head, and left coffee and paper both on the table as he got to his feet and walked to the telephone booths in back.

The phone books were on a slant-top table beside the booths. Parker looked in the local white pages and found only one William Dougherty listed, with the address 719 Laurel Road and the phone number Lloyd 6-5929. This was probably the right one, but it would be best to check.

He stepped into the booth and dialed. A woman answered on the third ring, and Parker said, "Detective Dougherty, please."

"Oh, he's at work. Call him at headquarters."

"Yeah, I'll do that."

Parker hung up, left the booth, and up front at the cashier's cage got directions to Laurel Road. He paid for the coffee he hadn't drunk, picked up the Buick from the no-parking zone out front, and headed away from downtown.

Laurel Road was in a section that should have been a suburb but wasn't. The city government, seeing all those taxable middle-income and upper-income people moving just outside the city limits into an area called Twin Knolls, simply shifted the city limits around a little, and very quietly Twin Knolls became a part of the city and its tax structure. The middle- and upper-income people promptly moved farther out, and lower-middle-income people like plainclothes detectives moved into Twin Knolls in their place.

Laurel Road was never straight. It curved away from a curving street called Camelia Lane, and kept right on curving, sometimes to the right and sometimes to the left. It looked like somebody's impression of a barber pole.

For the first few blocks, the widely spaced houses were large, sprawling affairs, split-level ranches with cantilevered sun decks over the carports. After five or six blocks, as the road meandered between more recent constructions, the houses began to get smaller and less ambitious, showing the result of city status. Shrunken flat-roofed ranches and narrow Cape Cods were clumped on smaller, less-landscaped lots.

Number 719 was far in, nearly at the end of it all. Two blocks farther on, Parker could see where the finished buildings petered out, and a half-completed house stood at the farther limit like a leafless tree.

He drove on by 719, glancing casually at it on the way by. It was a Cape Cod, with an A roof slanting front and back. A playpen was on the scraggly lawn, and the garage doors gaped open, exposing an empty interior. The curtains in the dormer window upstairs showed that the attic had been finished off into a room or rooms, which implied more than one child for Detective Dougherty.

Parker drove down to the end, where no work was being done on the half-completed house. He made a U-turn there, parked the Buick, and got out to walk over and look at what was done of the house.

There was no one working here today at all. Some clapboard siding had been put on, but mostly the exterior and interior walls of the house rose only as widely spaced studs of clean, new wood. This would be a Cape Cod when it was done; at the moment a ladder led to the upper floor in place of the staircase that hadn't yet been built.

Parker climbed up the ladder and looked around. This would be the attic. No internal partitions had been erected at all, but a full plywood flooring had been put down.

Sitting on a sawhorse over by the edge of the building, Parker could look down along the two blocks intervening and see Detective Dougherty's house and garage and driveway.

Parker lit a cigarette and waited.

4

It was a DeSoto, six or seven years old, that finally made the turn into the driveway of 719 Laurel Road. It rolled on into the garage, and Parker got to his feet and stretched.

It had been a longer wait than he'd figured. If Dougherty was running the murder investigation, he'd been on duty since at least midnight last night, but here it was almost four o'clock in the afternoon before he got home.

Driving a DeSoto. In a year or two, if he kept saving his pennies, he could trade up to an Edsel. And after that a Studebaker.

The sun was turning red off to Parker's right. Shadows were long, and yards and walks were deserted. Half an hour ago there'd been a flurry of homecoming schoolchildren, and in about an hour there'd be another flurry of homecoming fathers, but for now Laurel Road was empty.

Parker climbed back down out of the half-house and across the planks and dirt to the street. He left the Buick where it was and walked down the two curving blocks to 719. He went up the walk and rang the front doorbell. The lawn here was in bad shape, and the aluminium storm door had an aluminum D in the middle of it.

Detective Dougherty's wife opened the front door. Parker knew it was the wife because Dougherty surely couldn't afford a maid. She looked at him, faintly worried, faintly apologetic, faintly distracted, faintly present: the manner of the little housewife to the stranger at the door.

Parker said, "I want to talk to Detective Dougherty."

Now she was more worried, more apologetic. "I don't think—"

He knew she wanted to get across the facts that her husband was sitting down to warmed-over roast and planned to go straight to bed after that, but she didn't know how to say it all in the blank polite bloodless phrases to which the circumstances had her limited. He broke in while she was hunting around for more words, and told her, "It's about the case he's on, the Ellen Canaday case. You tell him that."

Now she had something specific to do, she was obviously relieved. She said, "Wait here, please," and shut the storm door. But she was afraid of offending him somehow, so she left the inner door open, and Parker could look directly into a small living room bulging with sofa and littered with copies of *The Saturday Evening Post.*

He waited a couple of minutes, and then Detective Dougherty himself came to the door. He was no more than thirty, but he had all the style of fifty; dressed in his undershirt and trousers and a pair of brown slippers, carrying a rolled napkin in his left hand, walking with the male approximation of a woman in late pregnancy. He wasn't stout at all, but he gave an impression of soft overweight. His round face was gray with lack of sleep and the need of a shave, and his dry brown hair had already receded from his forehead.

But it was all crap. His eyes were slate gray, and all they did was watch. The way he held his right hand, his revolver was still on his hip somewhere.

Parker stood loose, hands at his sides with the palms showing. When Dougherty pushed open the storm door, Parker said, "I'm glad I caught you home."

Dougherty said, "That's your car up the street, isn't it? The Buick?"

Parker shrugged. "It's mine."

"Come around to the side door." Dougherty pointed with the hand that held the napkin. "Around to the right there. It's okay to cut across the lawn."

Parker went around to the right, where there was a narrow space between garage and house. When he'd first driven by, he'd thought the garage was attached, but not quite. The roof overhang from both sides nearly met in the middle overhead, and a side door in the garage wall faced a side door in the house wall, but the two were separate buildings.

Parker moved down this cramped alley to the side door, and a minute later the door was opened by Dougherty.

Four steps led up to a closed door. Going to the left instead, a flight of stairs led down to the basement. Dougherty, standing up on the steps in front of the closed door in order to leave room for Parker to come inside, motioned toward the basement and said, "We can talk down there."

Parker went first. Dougherty shut the side door and went down after him.

The basement had been half converted to a game room or family room or some such thing. Vertical wood paneling covered the walls and formed a partition separating this part of the basement from the part with the utilities in it. Nothing had been done to make a ceiling yet, but over in a corner a few squares of vinyl flooring had been put in place over the original cement. For furniture, there was a pingpong table, plus a bulging sagging scratchy-looking sofa and a card table and some folding chairs.

Dougherty said, "The sofa's too uncomfortable. Let's sit at the card table. Take off your coat, why don't you?"

"I won't be staying long."

Dougherty shrugged and said, "Well, sit down a minute anyway."

They sat across from one another at the card table. Parker sat leaning back, his hands at rest in his lap. Dougherty leaned forward with his elbows on the table.

Dougherty said, "My wife tells me you have information for me. On the Canaday case."

"Something like that."

"You wouldn't be here to give yourself up, would you?"

"Not me."

"I didn't think so. But you *are* the man found at the scene of the crime."

"Probably."

"And you're here to tell me you didn't kill Miss Canaday, I should concentrate on others of her friends."

Parker shrugged. "I don't care what you do," he said. "I want a list from you, that's all."

"You want from me?"

"Boyfriends, all kinds. Anybody still living around town. Did she have an address book?"

Dougherty took his elbows off the table. "Let me get this straight," he said. "You want to ask *me* questions?"

"That's right."

Dougherty shook his head. "You don't look the type," he said. "You look too smart for that sort of thing."

"What sort of thing?"

"You're going to go do it yourself, am I right? You're going to find your girlfriend's murderer and bring him to justice all by yourself."

"Not me."

"No? What, then? I already know you didn't kill her, if that's what's worrying you. You'd been living with her a couple of weeks, neighbors identified you. You didn't make the phone call, the timing is wrong. You wouldn't have had to kick the door in if Miss Canaday was still alive. I imagine you'd be interesting to me in a number of other ways, because otherwise you wouldn't have run off like that, and I'd like to know what all those guns were doing in that closet, but I'm not sold on you for murder. You wouldn't be connected with the robbery out at the stadium, would you?"

"I'm not connected with anything. If you already count me out, who do you count in?"

Dougherty smiled and said, "I don't see a reason in the world to tell you anything. What's your name, by the way?"

"Joe," Parker lied.

"All right, Joe. I'm engaged in a murder investigation. In

order to keep my pigeon from flying away, I've let the newspapers concentrate on the search for you. But *I'm* not searching for you, the robbery detail is. They figure you were probably in on the robbery at the stadium, or at least you know the people who were. The guns in the closet connect you definitely."

Parker said, monotoned, not trying to convince Dougherty but just getting it said so it could be done with and out of the way, "I had nothing to do with the robbery. I went in and saw her there killed, and when the cop opened the closet door I saw all the guns in there, and I figured I'd be the fall guy so I ran."

Dougherty nodded. "That's bound to be your story, sure. But I'm not the one to tell it to. You want someone from robbery detail."

"I want Ellie's boyfriends."

Dougherty shook his head. "You've got to be kidding. You've got to have some other reason to come in here."

Parker said, "You're at a dead end on the killing. Robbery detail is at a dead end on the heist. Give me a couple answers, toss me in the middle of it, maybe I stir things up."

"You muddy the waters, you mean."

Parker cocked his head. "You want to go up and tell your wife anything?"

"Like what?"

"Like don't leave the house. Don't take the kids anywhere. You weren't dumb enough to have her phone the precinct, were you?"

"No, I wasn't. You haven't killed anybody yet, and you've got no reason to kill me. I'm in no hurry to arrest you for anything, because I'm working on a murder case and you connect somewhere else entirely. My wife and kids are going next door for a visit."

"Bad."

Dougherty said, "Don't pressure me. I won't pressure you and you don't pressure me. Why are you still in town?"

"I want names," Parker said.

"You won't get them from me. Could it be the actual killer

knows something? Something about the robbery, maybe. You can't afford to have him talk to the police; he might try to trade information for a lesser charge."

"I'll give him to you," Parker said. "Alive and talking."

"You don't make any sense at all," Dougherty told him. "Why do you want him, if not to kill him? What makes you think I'll give you any information?"

"You're too exposed, Dougherty. You know my arguments."

Dougherty glanced at the ceiling. "You mean my family? I don't believe it, it's too strong a reaction. You can't want information that bad."

"I do. My friends and I do."

"You touch me, or my family, and the force won't rest until you're found."

"You mean they'll start looking? They're just kidding around up till now?"

Dougherty gnawed his lower lip. "There's no point involving them in this," he said. "We should be able to work this out between us, just the two of us. Leave my family out of it, leave your friends out of it, leave the force out of it."

"Then what?"

"If I give you names, you've got to know I'll have those people put under immediate surveillance. If you show up to ask questions, you'll be grabbed."

"Let me worry about that."

Dougherty chewed and chewed on his lower lip. He didn't seem worried, just thoughtful. "I haven't got this figured yet," he said. "I believe you, you think this is important. Important to you, I mean. I believe you, you'll do whatever you have to do to get what you want. What I don't understand is why you want it, or why it should be so necessary."

Parker shrugged. "Never mind me. The point is, what do you get out of it?"

"If I give you names, they won't do you any good. You can't get near any of the people I mention without being arrested. If I don't give you the names, you'll probably cause me trouble of

66

one sort of another just to let me know you don't make idle threats, but all that can do is put even more heat on you. I don't see where you stand to gain."

Parker said, "Where do *you* stand to gain?"

Dougherty seemed to consider. "If I bring you in," he said slowly, as though talking to himself, "and it turns out you *are* connected with the robbery, it might even mean promotion for me, to second grade. If I let you go, knowing nothing about you but the license plate of the Buick, which surely won't do me any good, it won't help to announce to my boss I had you and lost you."

Parker said, "Don't figure you've got the choice."

Dougherty smiled thinly. "You have at least two guns on you, handguns of one kind or another, in your overcoat pockets. I have my pistol in a hip holster tucked into my back pocket. I'm the fastest draw on the force with the pistol in that position."

"You don't want to take the chance,"Parker told him. "Not here."

"That's true. Not if I don't have to." Dougherty spread his hands. "You haven't come here to cause me trouble, that's obvious. You have a request, that's all, and it's up to me to say yes or no. What if I offer you a trade?"

"What kind of trade?"

"Why do you want him?"

Parker considered. After a minute he said, "He has something I own, something he took with him. I want it back. When I find him, I'll take it back and then give him to you."

"What if it's the other way around? *I* find him, and give you back what he took."

"It wouldn't work that way."

"What is it he has?"

Parker shook his head. "It's something of mine."

Dougherty gestured, pushing the question aside. "All right, forget that. I want to know what happened at Ellen Canaday's place last night, what your part of it was, detail by detail. I won't ask you about anything not directly connected with the killing. You give me my answers, and then I give you your answers. Fair enough?"

"Why not?"

"Fine. You were the one broke the door down, right?"

"Right."

"Why didn't you have a key?"

"I wasn't going to be staying there that long."

"Did you hear a scream, any noise at all? Is that what made you break the door down?"

"No. I didn't hear anything."

"Then why break it down?"

"I'd been gone ten minutes. Ellie was okay when I left. It figured something was wrong when I came back and rang the bell and she didn't let me in."

"Had you been arguing, fighting at all?"

"No, we'd been screwing."

Dougherty seemed a little troubled by the word, but he rode on by it, saying, "Had she said anything about being frightened of anybody? Anybody at all?"

"No, or I wouldn't be here talking to you."

Dougherty smiled. "Of course. Sorry. You say you were gone ten minutes. Was she nude when you left?"

"Yes."

"In what room?"

"The bedroom, same as when I came back."

"In bed?"

"Sitting up."

"Was she planning on getting dressed?"

Parker shrugged. "Maybe a robe or something. She was going to fry some eggs."

"She was planning to leave the bedroom."

"Yes."

"Did you lock the door when you left?"

"It's a spring lock, locks automatically. I shut it all the way."

"You're sure of that."

"Yes."

"All right. How long were you back in the apartment before the two police officers arrived?"

"Just a minute or two. I just walked into the bedroom, saw her there, looked around, and there they were."

"You told them you'd made the anonymous phone call. Why?"

"They figured me for the killer. I wanted to give them a choice."

"But how did you know there *was* a phone call?"

"I didn't. But two cops walk in, somebody probably called. And if they got the tip some other way, that could still throw them off balance, give them the idea I'd already notified headquarters for them."

"Why did you wait and talk awhile? Why not run for it right away? Did you have to wait for them both to be distracted or something?"

Parker said, "I already told you that. When I saw the guns, I knew there was trouble. The guns in the closet."

"You didn't know about them."

"No."

"All right, never mind that. Who introduced you to Ellen Canaday?"

"A guy with an alibi."

"You're sure?"

"I'm sure."

"I'd like to check him off my list."

Parker shook his head. "No soap."

Dougherty considered, then shrugged and smiled. "Well, that's all right. You've got nothing to offer me? Nothing I forgot to ask?"

"You're doing fine," Parker told him.

"I'm not so sure. Okay, come on along upstairs."

Parker let Dougherty lead the way. Upstairs had the feeling of a house normally full and unexpectedly empty. The rooms seemed to hum with emptiness.

They went through a tiny bright white kitchen with Dougherty's dinner cold on a white plate on the red formica top of a kitchen table with tubular chrome legs. Then through a dining room filled to the brim by a maple table and chairs, and through a little square of leftover space where the stairs went up to the second floor, and on into the magazine-littered living room.

There was a closet near the front door, and Dougherty opened it and took out a baggy suitcoat that matched the baggy trousers he was wearing. From its inside pocket he removed a black notebook and handed it to Parker. "First page," he said.

Parker opened the notebook. On the first page front and back, were nine male names. Five of the names included addresses. Next to three of the names were little checks. Dan Kifka's name wasn't there at all.

Dougherty said, "You need paper? Pencil?"

"Yes."

"Come along."

Dougherty led the way back to the dining room, while Parker, following him, riffled quickly through the rest of the black notebook and found all the pages blank.

There was a glass-doored secretary standing crammed into a corner of the dining room. Dougherty got a pencil and sheet of yellow paper from this and put them on the maple table.

Parker stood to transcribe the names and addresses. The room was too small and jumbled for him to want to pull one of the chairs away from the table and sit down. When he was finished transferring all the names and addresses and check marks to the paper he said, "What do the marks mean?"

"Those are the ones I've talked to."

Parker looked at him. "Talked to? Or cleared?"

Dougherty smiled gently. "You keep your secrets, Joe, I'll keep mine."

Parker shrugged. "It doesn't matter."

Dougherty said, "That's all you want, right?"

"Right."

They walked to the front door, Dougherty saying, "I wonder what my boss'll say about this."

"He'll say you should have taken me."

Dougherty shook his head. "Not me. The robbery detail will catch you."

"Maybe."

"Oh, they'll catch you. They're very good." Dougherty opened the front door. "See you around," he said.

"Good-bye," Parker said.

5

Daylight was fast fading when Parker came out on the roof. He looked around, saw no one, and moved off to his left. He stepped over a low wall defining where two buildings met, and kept moving.

He'd come up onto the roofs at the eastern end of the block, and the building he wanted was about halfway down. He passed clotheslines, passed a pigeon cote, passed a rumpled, frayed, faded blanket left behind by someone in a hurry. When he'd counted buildings and knew he was at the one he wanted, he moved to the rear and over the side and down the fire escape.

There was no light in the apartment at all, and both windows opening onto the fire escape were locked. Parker took a roll of Scotch tape from his pocket, ran some pieces of tape back and forth across one of the windows near the inside lock, and then took a gun from his overcoat and used the butt of it to tap the taped window gently until it cracked several times. It was reasonably quiet this way and didn't take too long. When he peeled some of the tape off again, pieces of glass came off with it, leaving a hole large enough for him to get his hand through and unlock the window.

He doubted there was a plant in the apartment at all, but just to be on the safe side he opened the window with slow caution and climbed in the same way. He could assume there was a police guard outside the apartment door, in the hallway out there, but other than that he should have the place to himself.

He did. The bedroom looked strange with one of the swords missing from the wall and with the messed-up bed, but the body was gone and so were the guns from the closet. The rest of the apartment was unchanged.

Parker went through it quickly but thoroughly. He wanted names. Male, female, it didn't matter. What he wanted to know was Ellie Canaday's life. It was someone from that life who'd come in here and ended that life, and taken the money; that was his mistake.

There were a couple of telephone numbers jotted down on the cover of the phone book, without any names or other identification. Parker wrote them down without expecting much from them.

On various papers here and there in the apartment Parker found four of the names he'd already gotten from Detective Dougherty, but no new names, and no female names at all.

Sometimes it was a bad thing to be devoid of small talk. If he'd had meaningless little conversations with her the last few weeks he might have learned something he could use now. But Parker couldn't stand meaningless conversations, couldn't think of anything to say or any reason to say it.

The only time he talked about the weather, for instance, was when it had something to do with a job he was on.

All right, the apartment was useless. Still, he'd had to check it out before going back to Dan.

He went out the apartment the same way he'd gone in and started up the fire escape again. He went half a flight, and an automatic boomed above him, a metallic sting went pinging and ricocheting around him, slicing off the metal parts of the fire escape.

He flattened himself against the wall, dragging the pistol out of his left topcoat pocket, and above him again the automatic boomed and the slug went whining and whizzing on down the fire escape.

The first shot is for time. Not even bothering to look up, Parker raised his hand up over his head and fired upward, generally in the direction from which the shots had come. With the echoes of that shot still sounding around him, he ducked away again, back down the fire escape.

He could hear the sound of running feet within Ellie's apartment as he went on by the window he'd broken. So the cop on guard duty out in the hall had heard the shooting and was coming to see what was happening.

Parker felt a cold rage pouring through him. The bastard was right there, right up there on the roof! It had to be him again, hanging around, hanging around, taking his stupid potshots at Parker just as though he knew what he was doing. Right up there on top of the goddam building, and instead of going up and taking the stupid bastard apart piece by piece until the money fell out, Parker was running like a rabbit the other way.

Because of the cop. Because the maniac on the roof was so stupid he'd stand up there and shoot off a gun with a cop on plant inside the same damn building.

So he was up there, and by rights Parker had him cold, but instead of having him cold Parker was forced to let him go. And more than that. He didn't want the law to get its hands on the silly bastard yet, either, so he was going to have to make a distraction, he was going to have to cover for the bastard.

He had to make it possible for the bastard to get away.

Cursing, raging, Parker went on down the fire escape, firing a couple of shots nowhere in particular in order to distract the cop's attention from the roof. Above, the cop had found the broken window and had become aware of Parker going down the fire escape and was hollering for him to stop.

The bottom was a square pit, a concrete hole spotted with dented garbage cans. A black metal door led into the basement of the building, through blundering darkness in which Parker cursed and kicked and hurried, and then to a flight of stairs, and up, and through another metal door to the first floor hallway.

He stopped running at the front door. The pistol went back into his pocket, he closed his overcoat, took a deep breath, and walked calmly out the front door. He turned to the right, and a block away heard sirens coming from the other way. But he was clear now.

And so was the quarry. No matter how stupid he was, he had to be clear now.

Ready for refinding.

6

Janey was a disappointment with her clothes on; still pretty, but young and dull. She was wearing a pink sweater that made her breasts look like hard and youthful buds and a green skirt that gave no hint of the round rump underneath. She wore neither stockings nor socks, and on her feet were rumpled loafers.

She opened the door to Parker's knock, saw Parker standing there in the hall, and said, "Oh, it's you. You might as well come in. We've got a whole convention going here."

"Think you'll need help?"

"Don't talk dirty."

Parker heard sounds of talking from the kitchen and went over there first. Negli and Rudd and Shelly were sitting around the kitchen table drinking beer and playing knock poker. They looked up when Parker came in, and Negli said, "You must have it by now. You couldn't of been gone this long and come back without it. They didn't swipe it from you again, did they, Parker?"

"In a little while, Negli," Parker said, "I'm going to use you for toilet paper."

Shelly said, "What's the score, Parker?"

"Tied, nothing-nothing at the half."

Negli said, "Where've you been all this time?"

"Hiding from you." To Shelly and Rudd he said, "I've got to talk to Dan, I'll be back in a minute."

Negli had the last word, but Parker didn't listen to it.

Kifka, still holding his own with the virus, was sitting up in bed with two large yellow bath towels draped over his shoulders and torso to keep him warm. Clinger was sitting hunched in a chair like a bankrupt laundromat owner in his lawyer's outer office. Feccio, over at the window, was studying the world with an eye that reserved judgment.

Kifka looked up when Parker came in, and said, "Where've you been?"

"Getting started."

Clinger roused himself a little bit, and said, "I would never have expected it from you, Parker. Not you." He said it like it was Parker's fault the laundromat was bankrupt.

And it was; Clinger was right. Parker said, "I'll get it back myself, you want that. You want to help, fine."

Feccio, coming over from the window, said, "Parker, don't lose your logic. It could have happened to any of us. Some things you can't account for, you can't plan in advance."

Parker walked around the room with his arms swinging at his sides, his hands opening and closing. "The bastard can find *me*," he said. "He's got no brains, no sensible plan, he's a lousy shot, he's an amateur, but he can find me like *that*. And I can't find him at all."

Feccio said, "Dan told us. He's the one ambushed you last night."

"Twice," Parker told him. "Just this afternoon."

From the doorway, Negli said, "You keep up like that, Parker, you'll turn into a figure of fun."

Parker looked carefully at Feccio. "Turn your angelino off," he said.

Feccio's face darkened. "Don't start on me, Parker."

Kifka said, "Negli, what's your little problem?"

"My seventh," Negli told him. "Where's my seventh, that's my problem."

Kifka said, "We'll find it for you, okay?"

From his gloomy corner, Clinger said, "Squabble, that's what we need now. A nice long squabble." Rudd and Shelly had come in now and were just standing around.

Feccio said to the room in general, "Bob won't say anything

more, you got my guarantee." He looked at Negli. "My guarantee," he said.

Negli looked insulted, and walked over into a corner.

Kifka said, "What's the story so far, Parker?"

Parker told them of his afternoon: Detective Dougherty and Ellie's apartment and the madman on the roof. "I had to unload the Buick," he said. "And sooner or later that cop's going to get your name, Dan; you knew Ellie, and he'll come around here to ask questions, so we've got to find a different place to meet."

Feccio said, "Vimorama. We've got the run of the place. Dan could move right on out there now."

"Fine. All right with you, Dan?"

"As long as I got my Janey with me," Kifka said, "I don't care where I am."

Parker took Dougherty's list out of his pocket and gave it to Kifka. "You know any of these people?"

Kifka glanced down the list and said, "Sure. About half of them. This is the list you got from the cop, huh?"

"That's right."

Clinger said, "One thing I got to admit. I got to admit, Parker, you've got gall. You go to the *cop* to get your information."

Parker said, "He was the only one had it."

Rudd said, "One thing."

They all looked at him. Rudd was a silent workman type; it was a strange thing to hear him speak.

Kifka said, "What is it?"

Rudd said, "What we're talking about here is maybe twenty thousand bucks. Less than that. And financing out of that, maybe eighteen grand. For eighteen grand, Parker is walking into cops' houses, we're all hanging around here where a cop is going to show up sometime, maybe five minutes from now, and we're going to keep poking around in the same places where the cops are poking around. *They're* looking for the same guy as us."

"So what do you want to do?"

"Pack it in. I don't blame Parker, it could have happened to me, to anybody. But I say pack it in."

It was the most anyone had heard Rudd talk in years, so it had its effect. Much more effect than if Little Bob Negli had said the same things.

But Parker was aggravated. Somewhere in this dirty city there was a guy who had stolen two suitcases full of money from Parker. *And* shot at Parker twice. *And* killed the girl Parker was living with. *And* tried to set Parker up to take the fall.

What he wanted now was the appearances of logic and good sense. If the other six stayed active in this thing, then it was a simple sensible matter of getting the group's money back. But if they all quit, Parker knew he himself wouldn't quit, and he'd be going after the guy instead of the money.

He didn't like to catch himself doing things that weren't sensible, and that just aggravated him all the more.

He said, "Anyone wants to give up his seventh, just turn it over to me."

Negli rose to the bait. "Not you, Parker. Don't you even think it."

Kifka said, "*I'm* not going to pack it in. But face it, I won't be able to help much; I'm weak as a kitten."

Parker said, "Feccio? You in or out?"

"In, you know that. And so's Bob."

"Good. Clinger?"

Clinger shrugged and looked pessimistic. "It's good effort thrown after bad," he said, "but what can we do? Twenty thousand dollars is still and all and nevertheless twenty thousand dollars."

Feccio smiled and said, "Well spoken."

Parker turned around. "Shelly?"

Shelly grinned. "I got nothing else to do with my time," he said. "This might be interesting."

Kifka said to Rudd, "You're the only one doesn't want his seventh. You want us each to have a sixth?"

"I don't walk out alone," Rudd told him. "You people mess

around, with or without me, I'm still in the same trouble, it could still get back to me if you louse yourselves up."

"So you're in?"

"I'm in."

Parker said, "Dan, you've got to know more of Ellie's friends, names not on that list."

"Sure I do."

"Then write them down. We can't go near one of those nine unless we're pretty sure it's the guy we want. The reason I had to talk to the cop, I had to know which of Ellie's friends the law was on to and watching, and I had to know if they were on to you."

"Ellie hung round with different groups different times," Kifka said. He tapped the list of names. "Most of these are in a different kind of crowd from me. I know some of them, we've met here and there, but we're not buddies. Starting from these guys, the world these guys hang around in, it's going to take that cop a hell of a long while to get to me."

"Maybe."

Kifka shrugged. "All right, maybe. What about these phone numbers on the list here?"

"They mean anything to you? I got them in Ellie's apartment."

Kifka shook his head. "Not a thing. Let's check them out."

"Me," Clinger said. "My kind of proposition."

Kifka ripped that part of the sheet of paper off and handed it to Clinger, who went out to the living room to make the calls. Kifka took a pencil from the bedside table, wet the tip with his tongue, and said, "Other people Ellie knew."

Parker said, "With a grudge, if you know any."

"That I wouldn't know. Let me just give you the names."

Feccio said, "Then we go play detective?"

Parker said, "Something like that."

Rudd said, "We're looking for trouble."

"Don't worry, Pete," said Kifka. "This won't be as bad as you think." He shifted around in the bed and started writing names and addresses down on the paper.

For a couple of minutes there was silence, everybody sitting around waiting for Kifka to get his list finished. Clinger came back in and shook his head and said, "A pizzeria and a movie theater."

Parker said, "It figured."

Shelly said, "Who's for poker?"

They all trooped out but Parker and Kifka. Kifka sat on the bed, frowning in concentration like a wrestler trying to remember who's supposed to win this bout, and Parker went over to the window and looked out at the night-dark city.

He was out there, somewhere.

PART THREE

1

He was standing in a small square room with beige walls. The room was nine feet long, ten feet wide, nine feet high. Paint was peeling from the ceiling. A gray carpet covered most of the floor. The furniture was old and nondescript.

He was looking out the window at the night-dark city, feeling Parker's eyes. Somewhere, looking out from some other window in some other part of this city, were Parker's eyes, searching for him.

He didn't know Parker's name, didn't know his history, but it wasn't necessary. He had seen Parker. He had tried once to frame Parker, and twice to kill Parker. He had taken an awful lot of money from Parker, money which must connect Parker with that robbery out at the stadium.

He was terrified of Parker.

At the beginning of it, he hadn't really been aware of Parker at all. He'd known Ellen was living with another one, someone new, but his rage and hatred and sense of loss, all because of Ellen herself, had been so strong in him that he hadn't had the thought or the inclination to wonder about this new one, or care about him, or even consider him in his plans.

Except to wait for him to leave the apartment.

For two days he'd snuffled around that building, loping and looking, waiting for Parker to come out of there. He'd been out of town for a while, ever since Ellen had screamed at him that time, ranted and raved, cut him up with her tongue like slicing a piece of paper with a razor blade. She'd said things to him no one had ever said before in his life, things he would have killed a man for saying. She made fun of his triumphs, detailed his failures. She mocked his manhood, described the extent of his stupidity. She told him he was lousy in bed and worse out of it. She threw his electric razor out the window and told him to take the rest of his things and get the hell out of there. And when he went after her, driven beyond endurance, she'd run to the kitchen and grabbed a sharp knife out of the drawer there and held him at bay with it, screaming at him and taunting him all the time.

So he'd finally gathered up his gear and left the apartment, and she slammed the door after him. Standing in the hallway, he heard her slap the police lock into place. He had a key for the other lock, but not for that one.

He left town that same night, wound up in Mexico for a while. He knew Ellen would talk, would tell everyone how she'd routed him and why, and what she'd said to him, and how she'd held him off with a knife. He couldn't face them, face anyone he knew in that city, knowing they would know, Ellen would tell them.

After months in Mexico, humiliation and rage gradually hardened into something colder and more dangerous than either, and he'd finally come north again, knowing he wouldn't be able to rest until he'd paid Ellen back for everything she'd done to him.

He arrived Saturday afternoon. It was a cold fury that activated him, cold enough to make it possible for him to think, and to plan. He would even the score with Ellen, and he would do it in such a way that he himself would never be caught, because if he was caught and punished then that would negate the getting even, and Ellen would still be one up.

So he didn't just attack. He reconnoitered first, studied the apartment, and saw Parker going in and coming out. He saw Parker drive off with the truck and later come back in a cab. He was waiting then to see the extent of Ellen's perfidy. Was this stranger going to stay overnight?

Yes. Overnight and then some.

He waited. He'd taken a small room a few blocks away, and when he could stand it no more, when his eyes were closing and he was weaving on his feet, he went back there and slept, fitful dozing, plagued by bad dreams. It was fully night when he went to sleep, and still night when he drove himself up from the bed and out of the room and back again to watch Ellen's apartment.

He had begun by hating Ellen, but as the time went on, his hate expanded to include the stranger, too. Three days. Three days and three nights in that apartment there with Ellen. In bed with Ellen.

All the vicious things Ellen had said about his own prowess in bed came back to him, contrasting brutally against the silence of that apartment door and the slow inexorable moving of time.

Three days and three nights, and then at last the stranger came out. A big man he was, hard-looking, mean-looking. After all that time he didn't even seem pleased or satisfied; his expression was flat, emotionless.

The stranger went down the stairs. He waited, listening to the stranger's footsteps receding, then the door closing way down there at street level, and he was alone again.

His key still worked, and the police lock wasn't on. No, and not the chain lock either. He went in, moving fast, moving silently.

He knew she'd be in the bedroom. Where else could she be, the slut? Where else in all the world?

He came in and she was there as he'd expected, sitting cross-legged tailor fashion on the bed, a cigarette dangling from her loose mouth. She was half-asleep. She looked up and frowned at him, and she wasn't frightened. She wasn't even angry. All she did was act weary, disgusted, this-is-too-much-to-bear. "Oh, for Christ's sake," she said.

The details of his revenge had never been clear in his conscious mind. He had known only that he had returned to this city in order to even the score with Ellen. Now he was here, at the very core of Hell, at the brink of vengeance, and he felt an instant of utter panic because he had no idea what to do next.

He could see her eyes assessing his weakness, see her lips curling around the opening phrase of another cutting remark. He could see everything that would happen now; her verbal arrogance, his helplessness in the face of her, his clumsy, sullen, pathetic retreat.

Not this time.

His head turned this way and that, his eyes searched the room for something he didn't yet remember he remembered and then he saw the silver X on the wall, sleek and sharp.

It was too late for thought. Words were slipping from her mouth, ready to cut him.

He reached up his hand, and the silver X became a silver stroke, a diagonal slash separating the wall into metric feet, and the other slash was in his hand. He didn't know yet what he would do with it—though the hilt felt so perfect in his grip, so natural, so inevitable—and for an instant he just stood there, holding it above his head like a Goth on the way to Rome.

If even then she'd been frightened, everything might still have been all right. Even at that point, he might have been able to convince himself he had only taken the sword down to frighten her with, he meant no physical harm; anyone could see he wasn't the type.

But she wasn't frightened. Or if she was she made no sign of it. Instead she said with utter scorn, "You moron, what are you going to do with that? You never *could* stab me, not with—"

Knowing what she was going to say, knowing in advance all the ways she now meant to hurt him, he also knew he had to stop her. There wasn't any choice, none at all.

He lunged forward, and his right arm pushed ahead of him, and he impaled her forever on that red instant of time. The words remained unspoken, would remain unspoken ever after. The world tick-tocked on, and Ellen remained back there in that blood-red second, slowly slumping around the golden hilt.

It was as though he had stabbed her from the rear

observation platform of a train that now was rushing away up the track, and he could look out and see her way back there, receding, receding, getting smaller and smaller, less and less important, less and less real. Time was rushing on now, like that rushing train, hurtling him away.

That's what death is; getting your heel caught in a crack of time.

He had to get out of there, get away, but he couldn't turn his back on her. It was as though the sword wasn't enough to impale her there; she was being held also by his eyes, as though once he stopped staring at her she would live again, move again, speak again. As though, should he turn his back, catlike she would leap on it and bear him down under her weight.

Police. There would be police now. Had he left any clues?

He was wearing gloves; that was a lucky thing. He'd worn them because of the cold outside, not to cover fingerprints, but it came to the same thing. So he was safe there.

Anything else? Anything of him in this apartment, anything he hadn't taken away with him last time?

He studied the room and saw nothing, and then opened the closet door and saw the suitcases and all the guns.

All those guns.

And when he opened the suitcases—given the presence of the guns, he *had* to open the suitcases—when he opened them they were full of money. Bills and bills, green and green.

For a minute or two he forgot Ellen completely, sitting over there on the bed in a posture of contrition. He closed up the suitcases again, he grabbed one of the handguns at random and stuck it into his pocket, and he lugged the suitcases out of the bedroom, out of the apartment, out of the building.

His Ford, still grayed with the dust of Mexico, was across the street. He stowed the suitcases in it and clambered in behind the wheel, and looked out through the windshield to see the stranger across the way at the intersection walking back to Ellen with a package in his arms. He had a heavy, solid way of moving, as though he were made of metal. He looked inexorable, like fate.

These must be his suitcases, his gun. The closet had been full of the stranger's guns.

The stranger reached the building and turned and went up the steps and inside. He would go upstairs, find Ellen, and find the suitcases stolen and he would come looking.

In the rearview mirror he could see a telephone booth on the corner, all glass, held together by strips of green metal. He climbed out of the Ford and ran back to the phone booth, fumbling for a dime, fumbling for a plan. The thoughts clicked through his head like numbers through an adding machine. He was like a man on a bob-sled; later on he would have leisure to wonder just how he'd gotten down that bastard hill.

"Operator. May I help you?"

"Operator, there's a woman been murdered." His voice was a hush. "At 106-12 Longmans Avenue, apartment fourteen."

"What?"

"Get the police. Hurry! He's still there, the killer's still there."

"Sir, would you—"

"It's 106-12 Longmans Avenue, apartment fourteen."

"Your name, si—"

He hung up.

Returning to the Ford, he sat in the *back* seat, feeling clever. In the front seat he might be seen, but back here in the shadows and the darkness he could observe without fear.

Barely two minutes after his phone call a green-and-white prowl car shot around the corner and braked to a stop in front of *her* building. It stopped so hard it rocked a while on its springs, and two uniformed policemen clattered out and hurried into the building and out of sight.

His imaginings took him thirty times around the world.

The stranger came out, alone. He looked this way and that, and walked off down the street.

In the back seat of the Ford, he stared and ground his teeth and punched his hands together. What was wrong, what was wrong? Why did they let him go? With the dead body there, with all those guns in the closet, surely he hadn't been able to explain it all away so readily. Why had they let him go?

Or *had* they let him go?

What was this stranger? For the first time, it occurred to him to wonder what sort of man would have two suitcases full of money hidden carelessly in a closet, what sort of man would have pistols and machine guns on that closet floor, what sort of man would move with that square inflexible gait.

He followed because he was afraid to let the stranger out of his sight. He followed on foot because the stranger was on foot. Hurriedly he locked the doors of the Ford and then went off after the stranger, watching from a block back how the stranger planted his feet, how his arms swung like lead weights at his sides.

He trailed the stranger to the taxicab garage and beyond, until he saw that someone else was following the stranger too, a short, heavy man in a mackinaw, and then he hung farther back to wait and see.

When the stranger and the man in the mackinaw had their eerie conversation, he was close enough to hear without being observed. He heard them mention the name Kifka, and it seemed to him he could vaguely remember Ellen having mentioned that same name at one time or another. But aside from that lone name, the conversation had little meaning or interest for him.

Then the conversation ended, and the stranger went on, and the man in the mackinaw followed, until the stranger got into a taxi and went away and left the man in the mackinaw standing on the curb.

As soon as he was sure the taxi was out of sight, he came forward and talked with the man in the mackinaw and found he was unimportant, ineffectual, and harmless. But he did know the man Kifka's address; in that he had been lying to the stranger.

"Show me where he lives," he said.

"Sure. Sure." He was a weasel in a mackinaw, and his name was Morey.

He and Morey rode another taxi, and left it two blocks from

Kifka's address. It was awkward bringing Morey along, but he was afraid Morey might otherwise go to Kifka's place himself and warn the stranger of the man who was following him. It was best to bring Morey along.

Morey was full of questions until he showed him the gun and said, "Shut your stupid face." Then Morey was quiet. They crouched together in the driveway across from where Kifka lived, and waited. Morey had pointed out Kifka's windows, and they were all lit up.

The stranger had to be taken care of and then everything was done, and it was back to Mexico forever, this time with two suitcases full of money. It might be a little tricky getting the money across the border, but ways could be found. The spare tire full of cash instead of air, for instance. There were always ways.

He was dreaming of Mexico, and money, and didn't at first see the stranger come out the doorway across the street and start down the steps. When he did, he jerked his arm up, the heavy gun pointing, and Morey, the stupid one, shouted, "Hey!"

He turned the gun and blew Morey's loud head off. He didn't think about doing it, he just did it.

But it was too late to change anything. Across the way, the stranger was leaping for cover. He pushed Morey's falling body away and fired twice at the stranger, but missed both times.

And then the stranger shot back, and something stung his earlobe, like touching it for just a second with an electric wire.

He'd never had anyone shoot bullets at him before. It was terrifying. It was more frightening than he could have imagined.

He ran.

When he finally calmed down, he realized he shouldn't have run, that was the last thing he should have done. He'd lost the stranger now; the hunter could very easily at this point become the hunted.

He had to know where the stranger was, he had to. It was

necessary that he be behind the stranger, able to see without being seen, because the alternative was horror. If the stranger was not at all times in front of him, he would never know but what he was *behind* him.

He thought of fleeing to Mexico, right now, forgetting everything and only getting away from here, but he just couldn't do it. In Mexico, in Europe, anywhere on earth it would be the same; he was too afraid of the stranger to permit him to stay alive.

But the mistake had already been made. He went back, and Kifka's windows were now dark. The stranger had gone, of course, no telling where.

Behind him? He kept looking over his shoulder. Tendrils of ice kept creeping inside his coat to touch his spine. The back of his neck ached. His hands wouldn't stay still.

He went back to the rented room, taking a devious route, doubling back time after time, making wide detours around all pools of darkness. It didn't *seem* he'd been followed, but there was no way to be sure.

In the room, he arranged glassware on the window sill so it would fall and break if anyone opened the window. He pushed the dresser against the door. Even then, he slept only fitfully, his dreams chaotic, full of scarlets and ebonies, glinting with swords and guns, a-sting with bullets.

Most of the next day he spent in the room, waiting. He dozed sometimes, and stood staring out the window sometimes, and paced the floor sometimes. When, late in the afternoon, he finally understood that what he was waiting for was the arrival of the stranger, he forced himself into action. He couldn't just lock himself away in this cube on the edge of the world; he had to be out and around, he had to be *doing*. Whether or not there was anything to do.

He went past the place where Kifka lived, but didn't see the stranger there at all. The body of Morey was gone, too, with nothing now to mark the place where he had fallen.

(He couldn't really encompass the concept that he had murdered two people and tried to murder a third. He did these things because in their moments they were the only possible things he could do, but at no time did it seem to him that these actions were a part of the fabric of his personality. He was sure he wasn't the type; he did these extraordinary things because he had been thrust into extraordinary situations. In the normal course of events he would no more murder anyone than he would spit on the flag. His having killed Ellen, and then Morey, and then having tried to kill the stranger, were all atypical actions which he would not want anyone to have judged him by.)

He went past the place where Ellen had lived, and saw no sign here either that murder had been done within that building last night. On impulse, he parked the Ford in the next block and walked back.

The stranger had been living in there. Would he be in there again?

He went in, and up the stairs, and too late saw the policeman sitting on the kitchen chair outside the closed door. He couldn't go back down any longer, so he took the remaining alternative; he went on by the policeman and continued up the stairs. The policeman, reading a tabloid with huge black letters on the front, hardly gave him a glance.

There was no place to go but the roof. He emerged onto a flat deserted world with black tarpaper underfoot and the gray sky of late afternoon overhead. He walked cautiously across the roof, plagued by the idea that it wouldn't support his weight, that he'd crash through into the apartment below, and when he got to the front edge with its knee-high wall he squatted and looked carefully over, staring down at the street far below.

Would the stranger come back here? It seemed to him somehow necessary. Besides, there were only two locations where he knew the stranger might be, here and the Kifka place, so it was sensible that he should wait in one of these locations until the stranger should pass by again. Of the two, this was the better place to stay.

He wasn't sure whether he wanted to stay here because he thought the stranger *would* come back or because he thought the stranger *wouldn't* come back. Still, he kept watching the sidewalk far below and wondering if the gun in his pocket would fire accurately that far, straight down.

He wished he could go into the bedroom where he'd killed her and look around again. He supposed the body was gone, and that was a shame. Still, just the empty bedroom—he wished he could go in there and look around.

He squatted by the parapet, lost in his roiling thoughts.

A sound startled him, but he resisted the impulse to move, to make noise of his own. He turned his head and saw the stranger, far across the roof, just stepping off into thin air.

No, not into thin air. There was a fire escape back there, running down the rear of the building.

He reached with quiet haste into his pocket for the gun, but it was too late. The stranger receded downward, legs disappearing and then torso and arms and finally head. What a cold face he had!

He hurried across the roof just as quietly as he could, and got to the back edge just in time to see the stranger disappear into Ellen's apartment through the window down there.

Follow him? No, that would be far too dangerous. Sooner or later he must come out again, by this same route. All that was necessary was to wait, and this time not miss.

It didn't take long, but it seemed long. At last the stranger reappeared and started up the fire escape in the fading daylight, coming up toward the staring eye peering down at him past the straight line of the top of the automatic.

He fired and missed. Missed the way amateurs always do when shooting downward, aimed too high.

The stranger flung himself to the right, flattened himself against the wall down there. But still a target, still a target.

He fired again, and again he missed.

The stranger fired back, and shards of brick peppered his cheek as the bullet ricocheted by.

He couldn't stand that. If he lived to be a hundred and if someone shot at him with a gun every day until then, he would still never get used to it, never fail to give in to immediate panic. The stranger could be fired at repeatedly and still be alert and aware, still act in defense or offense. He would never know how the stranger did it.

For the second time he ran. Across the roof, pell-mell, all fears that he might fall through the tarpaper and the roof forgotten. He yanked open the door and pelted down the stairs, not noticing the kitchen chair standing empty in the hallway or the now-open door to Ellen's apartment. He ran on down, and out to the street, and a block away collapsed inside the Ford, frantic and ashamed of himself and out of breath.

After a while he went back to the room, and here he was now, still in it, a small square room with beige walls, the room nine feet long, ten feet wide, nine feet high. He was looking out the window, feeling the stranger's eyes, knowing he would no longer have the courage to go searching for the stranger himself, knowing he didn't have the courage to try to run away, knowing he could do nothing but wait here to be found.

He hadn't wanted any of this. It was all Ellen's fault, Ellen's fault. If only, if only . . . .

The room was getting smaller, meaner, dimmer. He couldn't stay here forever, he couldn't wait here indefinitely like this.

He deserved some time off. The tension had been so great for so long, it was about time he relaxed, forgot about things, found some way to amuse himself, distract himself.

He pulled the dresser away from the door and went out to the hall where the pay phone was. He called a friend of his, a guy he'd known in the old days, who said, "When did you get back from Mexico, man?"

"Just a couple days ago. You doing anything tonight?"

"Naw, you know."

"Why don't we take in a movie, have a couple beers?"

"Sure thing. Come on over. Say, wasn't that something about Ellie?"

"What? Oh, yeah. It sure was. Be right over."

He hung up, having made the mistake that would kill him.

2

Detective Dougherty wasn't at all sure he'd done the right thing. The *smart* thing, yes, there wasn't any doubt of that, but the *right* thing? Maybe not.

Driving downtown to talk it over with the lieutenant, Dougherty allowed himself little fantasies in which he got the drop on the man who'd called himself—obviously lying—Joe, in which he captured Joe, bested Joe, worsted Joe. In the cellar there, sitting as calm and deceptive as W. C. Fields playing poker, and then all at once—like Fields producing a fifth ace—whipping the pistol out and crying, "All right, hold it!"

In the dining-room, as Joe copied down the names, distracted . . . .

At the front door, as Joe turned to leave . . . .

"He that hath wife and children hath given hostages to fortune; for they are impediments to great enterprises, either of virtue or mischief." Francis Bacon said that, whether he wrote Shakespeare's plays or not.

Detective Dougherty was a good enough detective to have been aware of all the opportunities Joe had given him to try for an arrest. But he was also a good enough detective to know they were all opportunities *given* him by Joe, not out of carelessness but as a challenge. Every opportunity given him deliberately to remind him of his wife and children, currently next door, safely out of the house but close enough still to hear the shot that would kill him. And *listening* for that shot.

That, Dougherty thought to himself as he drove downtown, is probably the most enervating, the most spine-softening, the

97

most weakening thing that can happen to a man: to know that his wife and children are sitting with cocked heads listening for the sound of the shot that will kill him.

If there had been no wife, no children, Joe would never have walked in and out so casually. Dougherty might have died or Joe might have been caught, but either way it would have *ended.*

Of course, he knew full well that if there had been no wife or children Joe wouldn't have handled it the same way.

"He used my weakness," Dougherty said to himself. In his own personal soul, in the part of him that wasn't a policeman, he hated Joe for that and would pursue him more for having done that than for anything involving the stolen gate receipts or the murder of Ellen Canaday.

He found a parking space now two blocks from headquarters and walked back. It was not quite night; one out of three or four cars passing hadn't turned their headlights on yet.

After five o'clock, headquarters always took on for Dougherty the harsh surrealistic pregnant look of an IRA armory. He went up the slate steps and through the rotting doors and down the green antiseptic-smelling hall. When he at last came into the crowded wooden office of the lieutenant, he felt as he always did when in this building in the evening: like an unambitious Javert, a dull Maigret.

The lieutenant looked like Eisenhower, except that he never smiled, and when he did open his mouth for some other reason his teeth were yellow-brown and rotten and separated by wide gaps. He pointed to Dougherty to sit down and said, "I did what you said to do on the phone. Now fill me in."

Dougherty filled him in, telling him in flat monosyllables what had happened, giving no reasons or explanations this time through but merely chronicling the events, as though reporting the plot of some movie he had seen.

When he was done, the lieutenant said, "All right, I see why you didn't try to take him; that was smart, that makes sense, in your own home and all. But why give him the list? It's legit, the real list?"

"Yes. I didn't have another list of names handy. Besides, since he knew the girl himself he would naturally expect to know at least a couple of the names on any list of her friends I showed him."

"Did he say he knew any of them?"

"No, of course not." But that was the wrong way to say it; the lieutenant looked offended. Hurriedly, Dougherty went on, "I figured it was best not to ask him, not agitate him."

The lieutenant nodded and mumbled something, then said, "Why give him a list at all? Why not tell him the list is here, downtown, you can't remember the names?"

"This way," Dougherty said, "we've maybe got some leads to him. We know for sure nine people he's interested in. He naturally knows we'll be looking for him to come around one of those people, but if he's in that much of a sweat to get their names that he'll come around to my house and brace me for them, I figure he's in a sweat enough to try to get past us to the people themselves."

"Why? What's he after?"

"I'm not sure. This whole thing has to connect with the stadium robbery some way. I'd say this guy Joe was in on the robbery and staying with the Canaday woman till the heat was off. It would be my guess that whoever killed the Canaday woman took something of Joe's away from the apartment and it would probably either be something that would expose Joe's identity or prove his connection with the robbery, or it was his share of the loot itself."

The lieutenant said, "Ah. Somebody robbed the money from the robber. That would make him boil, wouldn't it?"

"It would explain why he's so on the prod."

The lieutenant nodded. "So he'll *have* to go after the people on your list. If he wants his money back."

"If it is the money. It could be something else, something incriminating."

The lieutenant waved an impatient hand. "Whatever it is, he wants it back in a bad way. You were smart, Dougherty."

Dougherty smiled, but inside he was cringing. He couldn't

help himself, but whenever the lieutenant complimented him he promptly remembered that the lieutenant hadn't finished high school. It was an odd fact he'd learned nearly by accident several years ago, before he was even in plainclothes. He never thought of it other times, but whenever the lieutenant complimented him, told him he'd done a job well, he'd been thinking on his feet, gave him any kind of praise at all, some nasty voice within Dougherty's mind promptly spoke up and sneered, "Not even a high school diploma."

The lieutenant was saying now, "What you ought to do, you ought to get together with Robbery Detail, whoever's working the stadium job, tell them what you've got, then start running the mug shots. How's he compare with the composite drawing, by the way?"

Dougherty shrugged. "The way they always do. If you see the guy first, then you can see where the drawing looks like him. But if you see the drawing first, you can't see at all where the guy looks like it."

"Then get together with the artist, whatsisname, get together with him, help him make up a new composite."

Dougherty took a deep breath. "Lieutenant," he said, "I'd like to get switched off the Canaday case."

"You'd like to what?"

"Have somebody else take that over for me, will you? Put me on temporary loan with Robbery Detail."

The lieutenant's eyes narrowed and his mouth opened. Now he didn't look like Eisenhower at all. "You got a bee in your bonnet, Bill?"

It was a rare thing for the lieutenant to call him Bill; it usually preceded a chewing-out. Dougherty said, reassuringly, "I don't want to be the Lone Ranger, Lieutenant, honest to Christ, I'm not the Robert Ryan type."

"You just want to be in on it." When the lieutenant was being sarcastic, he wanted the world to know about it; he carved his words out of blocks of wood and bounced them off the floor.

Dougherty let the sarcasm thud by. "That's right," he said.

"I want to be one of the people that runs him down."

"You don't care who bumped poor little Ellen Canaday."

"Not for a minute."

It almost looked as though the lieutenant would smile. Instead he opened his mouth and rubbed the side of his forefinger against his top front teeth, a rotten habit he had. "Go ahead," he said. "Go on home and get some sleep for a change. When you get back here I'll have the paperwork through on you."

"Thanks, Lieutenant."

"You think you'll find him again?"

Dougherty smiled in anticipation. "I'll sure as hell look," he said.

3

Kifka lay like a Teuton prince on a hill of pillows. He was in
Unit One at Vimorama, the only cabin there equipped with a
telephone. Janey, in an excess of zeal, had glommed the keys
from Little Bob Negli and rifled the pillows from all the other
cabins, heaping them up in a white slope against the headboard
of the bed Kifka was arranged in till he was lying more on
pillows than on bed, and he looked like a madam in an albino
whorehouse. He felt like a turtle on its back, waving its legs
and unable to turn over.

Only two things were within reach: Janey and the telephone.
He was occupied with both, grasping Janey to him with his left
hand and holding the phone to his ear with his right. Into the
phone he said, "Buddy, if I wanted to tell a story I'd sell it to
the movies. Answer the question or don't, it's up to you."

The telephone said, "Face it, Dan, I'm curious. Ellie's just
killed a couple days ago, now you call up about her, naturally I
want to know what's going on."

"Nothing's going on." Kifka rubbed Janey against his bare
chest and winked at her. "I want to know who knew Ellie,
that's all. Who do you know that knew Ellie that I don't know,
you know?"

Janey made a face and whispered, "No new new no." Kifka
pushed her face down into the pillows.

The telephone said, "When it's all over, for Christ's sake,
then tell me, all right? I mean when it doesn't matter any
more."

Kifka said, "Sure."

102

"All right," said the telephone. "Let me think."

Kifka played with Janey.

The telephone said, "How about Fred? Fred Whatchamacallit, Burrows. You know Fred?"

"Yeah. I already know him."

"Oh. Well, how about women? You want to know girls that knew her?"

"Anybody."

"Rita Loomis. You know her?"

"No. What's her address?"

"Uhhhh, Carder Avenue, I don't know the number. She ought to be in the book."

"Right." Kifka poked Janey and motioned at the pad and pencil over on the dresser. "Rita Loomis," he said. "Carder Avenue." Janey went over reluctantly and wrote it down.

Janey stayed at the dresser the rest of the conversation and had two more names to write down before she was done, one with an address and one with a phone number. Then Kifka hung up and she said, "How much more of this, Dan? Can't you put that silly phone down for a while?"

He shook his head. "No." He felt time crowding in, too much time. It was yesterday afternoon that Parker had been ambushed outside Ellie's place, and since then there hadn't been a sign of the bird they were after. Last night they'd all moved out here and Kifka had started his phone calls while the others had gone snooping around after the people Kifka turned up. The nine on the cop's list they weren't bothering with yet, hoping they wouldn't have to. Around midnight last night they'd packed it in, and started again this morning. Now it was almost noon and nothing was happening. Kifka was getting irritated and impatient, and Janey was getting worse.

She said, "You could take five minutes away from the phone, Dan."

"Parker's right," he said. "I'll never get over this virus with you around."

"Body heat," she said. "It's got to be good for you."

"Sure." He made his voice sound aggravated, but he was

pleased by Janey. She was an odd thing to happen to Dan Kifka and he was having trouble getting used to it. Kifka was a big blond-haired heavy with two assets: strong arms and an ability to drive. He pushed a hack sometimes for bread and butter, and took what other jobs came his way, punching heads if he was paid to, driving for operations like the stadium heist. He was thirty-four and used to the idea of who he was, and not expecting anything like Janey to come waltzing into his life.

The way it happened, he was driving the cab at the time, and a fuzzy-faced youth with a nasal condition and Janey had flagged him and given him an address out in the suburbs. All the way out they argued back there, the two of them, sniping at each other, the youth injured in a haughty way and Janey coldly furious. While the cab was stopped at a light, she finally threw him out, pushing the door open, pushing him on out onto the cobblestones, chewing him out the whole time. The youth ended in a paroxysm of snippishness, slammed the cab door, and stalked off into the night. The light changed and Kifka turned his head and said, "You want to wait for him, lady?"

"Lady" was inaccurate. She was a girl, not a lady, young and tender as garden vegetables. She was wearing a pink dress with a lot of crinolines and petticoats and doodads and gewgaws, and she was enough to make strong men chew carpets. She said, "I wouldn't wait for that twerp if he was my Siamese twin. Drive on!"

He drove on, and three blocks later she said, "Stop at a nice bar, I want a drink."

The customer is always right. He stopped at a neighborhood-type tavern and she said, "I don't go in these places unescorted. Come with me."

He said, "You see how I'm dressed?" He meant wrinkled trousers and a brown leather jacket and a Humphrey Pennyworth cap.

She said, "So what?" and that was the end of it.

In the bar, over a glass of sauterne, she became a compulsive talker, telling him her own life story and everything she knew about the kid who'd just walked out on her. There was nothing

104

special about either; both of them college kids from one-family houses, on their own in a city bigger than their home towns.

What he was, after just a little bit of it, Kifka was bored. She paid for her own sauterne, glass after glass, but meanwhile he wasn't picking up any fares, so it was still costing him money. Eventually he figured the one sure way to get rid of her was make a pass, so he did, and forty-five minutes later they were in bed together at his place.

It had been going on for eight months now, with time out for her summer vacation from college when she'd gone home for three months. Kifka had figured that was the end of it right there, but come September and there was Janey again, twitching her rump with pink impatience.

At first he'd kept his own life story to himself pretty completely, but gradually he got so he trusted her more, and by now she knew everything there was to know about him.

Except how to cure him of a virus.

"Body heat," she said, getting it all wrong.

He pushed her away and said, "One more phone call, all right? One more guy on the list and I'm done."

"If you promise."

"I promise."

But just as he was reaching for the phone it rang. He picked it up and it was Abe Clinger checking in, saying, "Scratch two more off the list. Bill Powell and Joe Fox, both covered for the time."

Kifka repeated the names for Janey to cross off on the main list, and then he said, "Abe, we're running out. We got to go to the cop's list now."

"I anticipated," Clinger said. "Believe me."

Kifka gave him two names and addresses, and Clinger gloomily repeated them to make sure he had them right, and then they broke the connection.

"One phone call, you said," Janey reminded him.

"That wasn't it." He shoved her back and dialed another number.

The voice that answered was fuzzy with sleep, wanting to

know what time it was. Kifka told him it was practically twelve o'clock noon, and the voice said, "Man, I was up till all hours last night. This crazy cat just back from Mexico, he dropped around, we talked the night away; I don't think you know him."

"Never mind do I know him, did he know Ellie Canaday?"

"Sure! Hell, they used to go together, you know what I mean?"

Kifka held a hand up in the air for Janey to start paying attention. Carefully he said, "What's this guy's name?"

4

Abe Clinger was a businessman, not a crook. It was his nature to be a businessman, and only the force of circumstances had him temporarily playing the part of a crook, a temporary condition that had lasted now about twelve years.

Television was to blame. Television was a blot and a rotten thing, ruining the eyes of young America, an insidious monster in living rooms all across the nation, showing sex and sadism, people smoking and holding glasses full of beer, destroying the livelihood of honest businessmen trying to make an honest dollar even with the minimum wage going all the time up up up and taxes getting worse every year. Even with government intervention and payments for workmen's compensation and social security and all the rest of it, it might have been barely possible to keep an honest man's head above water, except for the rotten box, television.

Abe Clinger had owned a movie theater. But a *movie* theater, the real thing, with a kiddie matinee on Saturday with twelve cartoons and a Western and a chapter, and beautiful dinnerware given away to the ladies on Wednesday evening, and always a double feature plus cartoon plus newsreel plus coming attractions, changed twice a week on Wednesday and Sunday. A nice friendly neighborhood theater that was like an institution almost, like the branch of the public library or the post office substation, a part of the neighborhood.

Until television.

Then, to make matters worse, when he burned the theater down for the insurance he did several things wrong and he got

107

caught. His wife of twenty-six years, when she learned he'd borrowed to the hilt on his life insurance and was also letting it lapse because he was going to jail, divorced him. His two sons looked at him with disgust and reproach, said, "Pop", in long-suffering voices, and went away to change their names.

But in jail he met a couple of people who made a new life possible for him, and when he got out on parole after spending the minimum time behind bars he was pretty sure he would never be bankrupt again. There was always work in the armed robbery line for a man who looked like a businessman or a bookkeeper or a general manager or whatever in the office-type the job might require. Carrying guns always made him nervous nevertheless, and he was yet to fire one of them, but he understood it was necessary in this trade, like being a Democrat in his previous occupation. Still, the new line of work had its advantages, like no employees and no overhead and no long hours, and his blonde was a hell of an improvement over the former Mrs Clinger, and generally speaking he had no complaints.

Except he was not a detective. Snoopyfooting around after people's whereabouts was not his line of work, and not about to be.

So why? Parker and Kifka and the others were all doing it, working away at this like it was a sensible job of some kind instead of craziness. Pete Rudd last night had made an excellent amount of sense, but the others all talked him out of it, and if the truth be known, Abe Clinger wasn't in all that much of a hurry to kiss the money good-bye either. As he'd said last night, twenty thousand dollars is twenty thousand dollars.

So here he was, walking down a cold street with a gun in his pocket, playing detective like Lloyd Nolan in all the second features he used to show, looking for somebody to ask stupid questions, carrying a clipboard for a prop.

This was an apartment-house block, a long block used up on the right side by four massive-shouldered brick apartment houses, the front all acne'd with air conditioners. The one

Clinger wanted was third, with a fine old stone arch over the entrance, the building number carved into the keystone of the arch, the whole thing looking like an ad for Pennsylvania.

There was an elevator, slow, trembling, painted red inside. Clinger rode it to the seventh floor, found the door he wanted, and rang the bell. He was no longer self-conscious about giving the spiel, he'd already done it eight times in other doorways. This time, of course, was the first time with someone from the policeman's list, but if there was one person he looked not a bit like, it was Parker, so what was to worry?

A young man in khaki trousers and a flannel shirt opened the door and stood like his skeleton was disjointed at the hip. He said, "Yeah? Something?"

Clinger held his clipboard and ballpoint pen very prominently in front of him. He said, "Are you the man of the house?"

"Yeah?"

Apparently it wasn't just a question, but also the answer. Clinger said, "If you have a minute, I represent Associated Polls. We're running a little survey. This shouldn't take up much of your time at all."

"You wouldn't be selling nothing? Encyclopedias, nothing like that?"

"Word of honor, I am not selling a thing. You have a television set?"

"Sure."

Sure. Everybody has a television set. Ask a man does he go to the movies, see what happens. But everybody has a television set, even beatniks. It offended Clinger, it made him feel like the butt of a joke to have to play the role of a television pollster, but Parker was right that this was the best way to handle it. In any case, he couldn't think of any better way.

He said, "I could come in?"

"Yeah, sure, what the hell."

Clinger smiled his thanks and went on in.

From here on, it should be smooth sailing. The bit was, he would ask about television viewing habits, and in the course of it he'd find out whether the suspect was watching television this Tuesday night when Parker's woman was killed. If the suspect was, then he wasn't a suspect anymore. If he wasn't, a few sly questions might find out what he was doing, or, if the suspect insisted on being vague about his movements Tuesday, then Clinger would so report to Kifka, and someone else would try a different tack.

In any case, Clinger's part shouldn't take more than five minutes and was safe as houses.

Except for the two bulky men who got to their feet as he walked into the living room, took their hands from their topcoat pockets, and began to walk toward him. One of them opened his mouth and said something to Clinger about showing his company identification.

Cops. *Real* cops.

The gun in Clinger's pocket had never felt so heavy or so useless or so monstrous, like a boil on the back of the neck. Without the gun, at least it would be possible he could fast-talk himself out of this. Without the gun, at the very worst he could clam up and wait it out and eventually be given an opportunity to jump bail because they really didn't have anything on him.

But *with* the gun, he was already breaking a law, concealed weapons; they had him as easy as pie.

Jail. He remembered it—gray and bleak and boring, impossible to survive in twice. No money, no soft furniture, no blonde.

He turned and ran, side-stepping the man of the house, bursting through the doorway and into the hall again. Behind him, shouts and imprecations, thudding of heavy feet.

Running, he fumbled the gun out of his pocket, meaning to get rid of it somehow, somewhere. Down the elevator shaft, in the incinerator, out a window, just anywhere. If they didn't catch him with the gun in his possession, actually in his possession, he still had a chance.

Behind him, the cops had already seen the gun in his waving hand and had misunderstood his purpose in holding it. They had their own guns out, and when they shouted to him to stop

110

and to drop the gun and he did neither, they opened fire, the shots cracking out in the narrow hallway with a sound like mountains breaking.

Two bullets buzzed past Clinger's head, and he kept running. The third thudded into his skull, hit him in the bald spot like it was a target, and he ran down.

The husk of Abe Clinger skidded to a stop along the hall floor.

5

Little Bob Negli liked to drive, so he and Arnie bought a car with separately adjustable bucket seats. That way, Little Bob could sit far enough forward for his short legs to reach the controls, and Arnie could sit far enough back to be comfortable. Their life together was a lot of compromises and adjustments like that, and most of the time things ran smoothly.

Except for other people. If it had been just the two of them, no one else around at all, they'd never have had any trouble; they'd have worked everything out the way they worked out the seating arrangement in the car. But there were other people in the world, and now and again they caused trouble.

Like women. Sometimes Arnie got a hankering for a woman, and off he went to get one, and Little Bob had nothing to do but sit around and wait for Arnie to come back, with or without a dose. Arnie always chose the sloppiest, scabbiest, rottenest tramps in the world when he wanted a woman, so Little Bob always made Arnie go to a doctor for a checkup before letting him back.

And like men. Some men just irritated Little Bob, aggravated him like itching powder, and the first thing anybody knew he'd be starting a fight. With somebody like Parker, say, who'd kill you as quick as look at you. Arnie was always after Little Bob to watch his mouth, quit picking fights, quit acting like such a troublemaker.

So Little Bob was annoyed by the women Arnie picked to

112

sleep with, and Arnie was annoyed by the men Little Bob picked to fight with, but these two gripes were just about the only problems in their life together. It struck them both as a small price to pay.

Little Bob now sat in the car parked by a fire hydrant, waiting for Arnie to come back from another interview. Little Bob himself was too chancy a character to be trusted, going around asking questions of strangers. He'd be in a brawl within an hour, and that usually meant bad trouble. Being so small, he figured it wasn't up to him to fight fair. He kept a switchblade knife close to his left hand, and a .25 Beretta automatic close to his right.

That's why Little Bob was doing just the driving and Arnie the questioning. Again it was a compromise that worked out fine for both of them. Little Bob liked to drive, and Arnie liked to talk with people.

It was about two in the afternoon. Arnie had questioned four guys last night and five more this morning and had gotten nowhere. Two so far hadn't automatically eliminated themselves with the television gambit, and Arnie had passed their names on for Parker and Shelly to check, but apparently neither of them had been the guy they were after. So now they'd run out of the other names and were working at last on the original list the cop had given Parker. Arnie was in there talking to the first of them now.

Little Bob wasn't pleased about it. It figured the law was watching this place—waiting for Parker to show up. Little Bob hadn't been able to spot them yet, but they had to be somewhere around. And what if they decided to question Arnie? That would be just one more thing he'd have against Parker.

Waiting for Arnie, Little Bob took the time to nurse his grudge against Parker. Parker had manhandled him back at Vimorama, but that was nothing. The big gripe was that Parker lost the goods, caused all this trouble. Because of a woman, naturally. Shacked up with some woman he doesn't know anything about, and naturally she's got enemies, and the whole

113

thing follows like the night the day. Why they'd trusted Parker with the nick in the first place he'd never know.

Looking out the windshield, thinking about Parker, Little Bob suddenly saw Arnie coming out of the apartment house ahead in the hands of the law.

It had to be law, two stocky types with fat faces and cheap topcoats. They flanked Arnie on either side, and the way his hands were behind his back had to mean they'd put the cuffs on him. The cops had been *inside*.

Damn Parker!

Little Bob shifted into drive, and the car inched forward close to the curb. He knew Arnie would have seen him coming, out of the corner of his eye, and it all depended now on timing.

There were parked cars up there. Little Bob angled out around them, glided forward, and leaned way over to his right to unlatch the passenger door and then, as he braked at the spot between two parked cars, and as Arnie made his move, Little Bob shoved the passenger door open and reached out to drag Arnie aboard.

Arnie had moved right, lunging backward at first to throw them off balance, then bumping both and crashing on through and between the parked cars where there was just enough room for him, running like an ice skater about to lose his balance because of the handcuffs holding his hands behind his back, and just as he dove for the open door of the car the booming started, and Arnie's face, as he dove still in midair, turned suddenly gray, and he crash-landed half in and half out of the car, and Little Bob's reaching hand, clawing across Arnie's face, felt the flesh pasty and soft.

Arnie was sliding backward out of the car, his cheek scraping back across the red upholstery of the bucket seat. The booming went on, and the windshield starred as a bullet went through, and there was nothing for it but to hit the accelerator and get out of there, leaving Arnie behind dying or dead; nothing else to do, no other way.

Within eight blocks, twisting and turning, he knew he was

114

clear. He slammed the car into a parking space and got out, leaving it there forever.

Dead or dying. The whole setup shot now, shot forever. There'd never again be a team like Little Bob Negli and Arnie Feccio.

And all because of Parker, that stupid bastard, that clod, that mindless bungler. Parker was the one to blame.

"I'm going to get you, Parker," he said. He threw the car keys into a garbage can and walked on.

6

For a man who hated to talk, being a polltaker wasn't an easy job. Pete Rudd hated to talk.

Like Abe Clinger, Rudd had come to his profession as a second choice. He'd started as a carpenter and cabinet-maker, and he did slow and careful work with very expensive wood. It was difficult for him to find good materials, but that wasn't enough to drive him out of the business. What drove him out was the lack of good customers.

Outside every large city in the country there is a highway flanked by shopping centers and discount stores, like a row of roofed-over city dumps. In these places, in plastic or cheap wood, shoddily assembled, barren of design, can be found the sort of product Pete Rudd was making slowly and carefully in a drafty workshop with concrete floor. Rudd's work cost five times what the competition was charging, and would last ten times as long. He came close, a few times, to starving to death.

He made a trunk for a customer one time, a special sort of trunk with a hidden inner compartment. The customer offered him extra money to keep the secret of the trunk a secret, and Rudd refused it; it was ridiculous to pay Rudd to be silent. When the customer came back with an illegal proposition for Rudd two months later, Rudd looked into his empty cash register, leafed through his unpaid bills, and joined the mob that took the Regal Electronics payroll in Mobile. His job in that one was to dummy up the interior of a truck with a fake partition behind which five men could hide.

For a while after that, the occasional robberies helped to keep his woodworking business solvent, but gradually he was doing less and less woodworking, because while the robberies solved his lack of money, they didn't solve his lack of customers. By now the woodworking was down to a hobby and an easy cover of respectability; Rudd's main profession was heisting.

The nice thing about the job, for him, was that it practically never required talking. Other people, people like Parker, did all the planning and explaining. They told Rudd what they wanted him to do, and he did his part not caring about how it fit into the general scheme, and when the job was over he took his split and went home.

Sometimes things went wrong, jobs turned sour. When that happened, he went home without any money, but he still went home. He'd never been touched by the law, and he saw no reason why he ever would be.

Which was one of the reasons he didn't like hanging around here in this city this time. There was law all over the place. The take, his share of it, was only around twenty thousand dollars anyway. He could get that somewhere else before the year was up.

But the others were all in it, so he had to be in it too. So here he was, carrying a clipboard, walking around asking dumb questions, checking back with Kifka every once in a while to tell him how he'd done so far and to get another trio of names, and then off again.

This one was a walk-up, a furnished room. Rudd doggedly climbed the stairs and knocked on the door, and after a minute it was opened by a tall, broad-shouldered young man with a deep tan. He looked like a halfback on a college football team. His expression was suspicious as he said, "What is it? What do you want?"

Rudd knew immediately the television gambit would be no good here; in a furnished room like this, this guy wouldn't have a television set. So he said, "Radio."

The guy frowned. "What? What's that?"

"Radio," said Rudd. "I'm from Associated Polls, we want to know when you listen to the radio."

"Radio? I don't listen to the radio, I just moved in here."

"We want to know," Rudd said, pushing it, "what programs you listened to on Tuesday night. Did you listen to the special—"

"Tuesday night? What about Tuesday night?"

"We want to know—"

"Come on in here. Come on."

Rudd went in and the guy shut the door. It was a small square box of a room, badly furnished.

The guy turned around from the door and hit Rudd with his closed fist on the side of the head. Rudd stumbled and fell over a chair, and the guy came after him and kicked him in the small of the back. "Who sent you?" he said. "Who sent you here?"

After a while, Rudd told him.

7

Ray Shelly was an easygoing sort. Only once in his life had he hit anyone in anger, and that was a major in the United States Army. Shelly at the time was a private in the United States Army, and in the major's private bed, and very close to the major's wife. The major, returning unexpectedly and finding his wife and Shelly in bed together, had taken one look at the size of Shelly and had then started to beat up on his wife instead. He got to hit her twice before Shelly flattened him. Shelly got six months stockade and a bad conduct discharge out of that, the major got a transfer to a base where his presence wouldn't cause so many snickers, and his wife got a change-of-life baby.

Sitting on the sofa in the living room of a guy named Fred Burrows now, Shelly thought about that time and wondered how the major was treating his kid. The kid would be eight years old now. Nine. No, eight.

Parker was doing the talking for both of them, so Shelly didn't have to waste any time listening. He and Parker had already gone through this routine four other times, and it hadn't come to anything yet, and he didn't really expect it would come to anything this time. This Fred Burrows looked about as dangerous as a ladybug, soft and plump and scaredy-cat. He blinked a lot.

What they were supposed to be, him and Parker, they were supposed to be law. Parker always had these identification cards, driver's licenses, discharge photostats, credit cards, all these bits and pieces of paper he kept assembling with other people's names on them, and when it was necessary for him and Shelly to ape law, out he came with a couple of identification cards that said POLICE all over them. They weren't for this city, but nobody reads a cop's card that close.

This was their fifth call. Whenever Feccio or Clinger or Rudd ran into somebody they couldn't fix with the television questions, they passed the word on to Dan Kifka back at Vimorama, and Kifka passed the word on to Parker and Shelly, and Parker and Shelly went visiting in law face. The dodge was, they were investigating the murder of Ellen Canaday, and they wanted to know where this particular gismo was on Tuesday night. After they got the answer they checked it if necessary, and wound up scratching another name off the list.

Like this boy Fred Burrows. Shelly didn't have to listen to the questions or the answers; he already knew you could scratch Fred off the list. But Parker was going through it all anyway, just like it mattered. Parker was thorough, and Shelly recognized that was a good way to be. Not for himself, though; he was too easygoing to be thorough.

Parker at last gave the high-sign they were finished, and Shelly got to his feet, stretching his back and twirling his hat like any harness bull anywhere. Parker told Fred Burrows, "We'll be in touch. Don't leave town." Shelly scratched his nose to hide a grin, and they went on out of there, leaving Fred Burrows smiling painfully in the doorway.

Out on the street, Parker said, "He's out."

"I knew that all the time."

Parker shrugged, looking around. "We'll go back to Vimorama," he said.

"Sure thing."

They walked down to Shelly's car, a seven-year-old Pontiac with a five-year-old Mercury powerplant and Ford pickup transmission. It looked like hell, and it sounded like hell, but it also went like hell.

Driving out to Vimorama, Parker said, "I don't like the smell of it. It's going to be one of the cop's nine."

"We'll know pretty soon."

"I don't like going near those nine. What if the law grabs anybody that comes along, doesn't just wait for me?"

Shelly shrugged and said, "If it was me, I'd give myself up peaceful as could be and say I was doing it for a joke. They might have me on some kind of misdemeanor, gaining entry under false pretenses or something like that, but that couldn't hurt me none. I'd just wait them out."

Parker shook his head. "I just don't like it," he said.

Out at Vimorama, they took the car around on the gravel driveway to the rear of the property, where it couldn't be seen from the highway. They got out and started crunching back across the gravel to Unit One, where Kifka was. Shelly walked on the right, Parker on the left.

Shelly, glancing to his right, saw Little Bob Negli suddenly pop out from behind one of the cabins over there. He had a gun in his hand, a little gun, shrimp-size like himself.

Negli shouted, "Shelly, move over!"

Shelly had been starting to grin. Now he started to frown instead. "Bob, what the hell are you—"

"Move out of the way!"

Then, beyond Negli, Shelly saw someone else, a young guy, heavyset like a football player, loping forward between the cabins. Everybody had a gun in his hand all of a sudden; the young guy's hand bulged with a .45 automatic.

Shelly shouted and dragged his own pistol out from under his coat. But Negli must have misunderstood. He shot Shelly three times.

8

After the man named Pete Rudd told him everything he wanted to know, he knocked Rudd out with his fist and got ready to leave here.

It had been pleasurable, forcing Rudd to talk. The last time he'd felt that way, free and exalted and as strong as a redwood tree, was back in college in football season. Hitting a man was like hitting a line; exulting in your own strength and the chance to bruise and push and bull your way through.

Rudd had been troublesome. It had taken a long while to break him down, and he worked up quite a sweat doing it. So, as always after prolonged exertion like that, he spent a while in the shower. Here, in this miserable place, the shower was in the bathroom down at the end of the hall. It wasn't even a proper shower; he had to stand up in the tub, with a shower spigot over him and a plastic shower curtain constantly blowing inward and wrapping itself around him.

When he got back to the room, Rudd was still out, sagging in the chair to which he'd been tied with shoe-laces and strips of his own shirt.

He packed quickly, but not hurriedly. There was no reason to hurry now. He knew what had to be done, and when it was finished he would go to Mexico as planned. He felt very peaceful now, with everything mapped out that way, and having had a good workout and a good shower afterward.

Various things that Ellen had said to him at one time or another, things about his abilities with women, kept trying to creep into his consciousness, but he was feeling too good to let such nonsense bother him. He pushed those memories to one side, old ballast he no longer needed.

When he was done packing, he had four suitcases, his own two filled with his clothing and other possessions, everything he owned in the world, and the two filled with money. As an afterthought he opened one of the money suitcases and took out handfuls of cash, stowing it around in his pockets. If by any chance he should be temporarily separated from his luggage, he'd still have plenty of money.

He considered Rudd awhile, and then decided to leave him there and do nothing further to him. What was the point, anyway? No one else would be coming along, not for a while. And there was no need to kill this man Rudd; he wasn't a threat. None of them were threats, only the leader, the one who'd been living with Ellen. *He* would follow to the ends of the earth. Yes, but kill him, and the others would all slink off like whipped dogs.

He made two trips down to the car, carrying the suitcases. The second time, he carefully locked the room door behind him. Good-bye, room. He wouldn't be coming back to that place.

He drove the Ford out 12N, as Rudd had told him, and eventually saw Vimorama on the right. Seeing it, he felt his first moment of doubt; it really did look deserted. But then, going by, staring at the place, he caught a glimpse of a car parked way in the back, behind all the cabins. So Rudd hadn't been lying.

He *couldn't* have been lying, not by then.

He let the Ford glide on by Vimorama and stopped about a quarter mile farther down the road, where there was parking space along the verge. He walked back, feeling the guns in his pockets. The gun he'd been using up till now had only five bullets left in it, as he'd learned when he finally figured out how to get the clip out of the butt. Rudd had been carrying a gun too, a different kind, what they called a revolver. It held eight bullets and was fully loaded. With two guns now,

123

bolstered by the feeling of strength and power, he strode rapidly back down the road toward Vimorama.

Ahead, he saw an old Pontiac take the turn, drive in past the Vimorama sign. He quickened his pace.

There was a gas station on the left, and then a bit of woods before Vimorama began. He walked past the gas station and then plunged into the woods.

The trees were tall old pines, widely separated. A rust-brown mat of dead pine needles covered the ground. It was dark in under the trees, and all sounds were muffled. He took the automatic out of his right-hand topcoat pocket and walked along peering and searching, frightened in spite of himself.

The Vimorama cabins were off to his right. He turned that way and came out from under the trees, and ahead of him were the cabins and people. A short man directly in front of him, maybe ten yards away, was facing the other way. Beyond him, possibly twenty yards farther on, walking along the gravel driveway, were two tall men, and the one on the far side was the leader, the one he wanted.

They were all shouting at each other, and he suddenly saw he was coming into the middle of a situation he didn't fully understand. The short man had a gun in his hand, and all at once he started shooting at the leader and the other one. The leader ducked away and the other one fell to the ground.

Was the short man on his side? He came running forward, shouting, "Get him! Get that tall one!"

The short man spun around, open-mouthed, and fired again. At *him!*

He yelled and dove away, rolling the way he'd learned in college, bringing up at last behind a cabin, lying there awhile quivering with fear and rage.

He was enraged at everybody, but mostly at himself. It had happened again, as it always happened, as he knew it always would happen. A gun was fired at him, and he reacted with blind instinctive panic. He lost precious seconds, lost advantages, lost control of situations, only because of this stupid panic, and it hit him every single time.

124

Out of sight, the shooting was still going on. He crept around the other way, trying to see without being seen, hoping there would be some way to come up on everybody's flank. The shooting was sporadic, it almost sounded half-hearted in comparison with movie soundtracks, and it seemed to be moving here and there all around the cabins.

He came around the corner of the cabin and there ahead of him, looming in a cabin doorway like a Scandinavian god, was a huge naked blond man wearing nothing but a gun.

Everyone had guns.

He fired first this time, three shots from the automatic, and the naked man bounced backward into the doorframe and then jacknifed forward and sprawled out on the gravel.

Shooting. Shooting.

It sounded like it was all around him. It sounded like it was all *at* him.

He turned and ran.

He ran through the woods and across the gas station blacktop as the attendant there gaped open-mouthed at him, and ran full tilt along the road until he came to the Ford again. He pulled open the door on the passenger side because that was the side he came to first, and something hit the inside of the door and made a shock wave run up his arm, and a second later he heard the sound of the shot behind him.

He didn't even look back to see who was shooting at him. The woods were to his right. Leaving the car door open, he turned away and went crashing and blundering in among the trees.

9

Detective Dougherty could smell it in the air. Tension. Something was about to pop.

His original list of nine names had been expanded by now, and the men still working on the Canaday case reported that almost everyone they talked to had already been questioned by someone claiming to be from a poll-taking company. The descriptions of the pollster varied too widely to be just the normal bad memory of the civilian witness; there had to be more than one man doing the questioning.

The man who called himself Joe had friends with him, then. The others involved in the robbery at the stadium? But why would they stick their necks out for him?

Unless what Joe was looking for was more than his own share of the loot. Unless the Canaday killer had the whole bundle.

Dougherty could think of no other explanation. The man who had murdered Ellen Canaday had also walked off with the entire proceeds from last Saturday's robbery. Five to eight men had been involved in that robbery, according to the best estimates they could work up, and undoubtedly all of them were still in the city, looking for the murderer of Ellen Canaday.

It was as involuted and twisted as a Chinese puzzle. The police were looking for the Canaday killer. A group of professional bandits was also looking for the Canaday killer. And the police, to round it off, were looking for the professional bandits.

If the Canaday killer were looking for either the police or the bandits, then everything would be tied in the ultimate knot.

Well, they all had to start bumping into each other pretty soon. Too many people were milling around in the same restricted area; sooner or later they had to start making contact.

It began shortly after noon, and then it came twice in rapid succession. Two men were picked up when they came to apartments of people on the list Dougherty had given Joe. It had been Dougherty's idea to put men on duty inside the apartments instead of merely on watch outside. How would they know what they were watching for if the fake polltakers were people other than Joe?

Well, it paid off. Two of the pollsters were nabbed within ten minutes of each other.

But the news was as bad as it was good. Both men had tried immediately, and disastrously, to escape, and both had been shot down. One of them had apparently had some idea of shooting it out, but had died with a gun in his hand that he hadn't had a chance to use. The other had had an accomplice in a white Chevy II with red upholstery, and had almost succeeded in getting into the car and away. One of the arresting officers fired at his legs, but did so just as the suspect was ducking, and the bullet struck him in the back instead. He was still alive when he reached the hospital, but in a coma and not expected to regain consciousness. The accomplice and the white Chevy II were being searched for.

Also, the ambulance the gang had used in the robbery had finally been found. And, downtown, a truck with a Renault hidden inside it had drawn the attention of a patrolman after it had remained parked in one spot for nearly a week; it seemed certain the truck and Renault had had something to do with the robbery. None of the three vehicles bore a single useful fingerprint.

The new composite drawing of Joe, done by the police artist with Dougherty's directions, had been identified by a cashier at the stadium as one of the men engaged in the robbery, if they needed any confirmation of *that*.

Then, at four-thirty, the phone on Dougherty's desk rang, and when he picked it up it was Engel, the detective who'd taken over on the Canaday case.

Engel said, "I think I've got something for both of us, Bill. Checking out a report on an old boyfriend of the Canaday woman's, fresh back in town from Mexico, and the boyfriend's gone, but he left behind a guy who just might be part of the robbery gang."

"Where is this? Is it Joe?"

"No, it doesn't look like the drawing. From the looks of things, this guy was doing the poll routine and the boyfriend tumbled and then beat the crap out of him to find out where the rest of the gang was hiding."

"The boyfriend's the killer?"

"It looks that way."

"And *he's* after the *gang*?"

"Yeah, I know. They're supposed to be after him."

Dougherty said, "This one's a lulu."

"Yeah. Anyway, this guy, he's got identification says his name is Peter Rudd, he got beat up pretty bad before he decided to talk, and now all he wants to do is just keep talking. He keeps telling us where the gang is, over and over."

"He does? Where?"

"Some place called Vimorama, out on—"

"I know where it is. I'll meet you there."

"Check."

Dougherty put in a quick call for two cars and a riot squad and ran downstairs as fast as he could go. He got to the street before the cars did and stood there fidgeting back and forth from foot to foot, quivering with impatience.

It occurred to him he'd forgotten to ask the name of the boyfriend, the one who'd killed Ellen Canaday. But it didn't matter. Who cared what that guy's name was?

The two cars came up out of the basement garage and paused for Dougherty to slip in beside the driver of the first car. "Vimorama," he said. "Out 12N."

"Siren?"

"No. Yes, till we get to the city line. Then cut it off."

City line. He wasn't even sure he had jurisdiction out at Vimorama.

Well, the hell with that.

The two cars screamed through the city and took the last couple of miles in silence, tearing along with the red lights flashing but no sirens sounding.

When they got there they saw it hadn't made any difference how much noise they made. There was no one around anymore to be disturbed by them.

There'd been a fight out here, but it was over now. A tall long-armed guy lay sprawled out on the driveway that went in among the cabins. He'd been shot three times, twice in the chest and once in the head, all from fifteen or twenty yards in front of him.

Over to the right a ways, there was a scene for Debussy to write a ballet around. A huge-chested blond giant as nude as the day he was born was lying dead on the grass, his head cradled in the lap of a cute little blonde girl wearing nothing but a pink half-slip. She wasn't crying or anything, just sitting there on the ground with her feet tucked in under her and the dead man's head in her lap, stroking his cheek with long, thin fingers.

Dougherty tried to ask her some questions, but she wasn't having any. She just sat there and didn't look at anybody or respond to anything. He told one of the uniformed men, "Call an ambulance. Tell them we've got a mental case. Catatonic."

Engel and more uniformed policemen showed up then in two more cars, and Vimorama was beginning to get crowded. Engel came over and said, "What's all this?"

"I don't know. I just got here myself."

"Is your boy Joe here?"

"Doesn't look like it. So far just these two dead ones and the girl."

"You ought to get her a brassiere or a coat or something."

Dougherty glanced that way, and then shook his head. "She's

129

in shock or something," he said. "I wouldn't want to bother her. Either of these your boy what's-his-name?"

Engel shook his head. "Naw. Mine's younger than this. Big like that one, but black hair."

Dougherty said, "What *is* his name, by the—"

Somebody shouted, "We found the car!"

Engel shouted back, "The Ford?"

"Yeah! Down this way!"

"Gray Ford with Texas plates," Engel told him. "The boyfriend's."

"So he's still around."

The two of them went walking down the highway to where the gray Ford was standing with the passenger side door hanging open. When they got there Dougherty pointed at the door and said, "Look like a bullet hole?"

"Looks like."

Dougherty glanced over at the woods. "Went in there, I suppose," he said. "Chasing each other. I don't suppose I'll ever find either of them."

Engel said, "Look at the back seat there. That's a hell of a lot of suitcases for one man."

Dougherty looked at the suitcases and smiled.

PART FOUR

PART FOUR

1

When Negli started shooting, Parker dove for cover. None of it made any sense to him, but this was no time to stand around and wait for explanations.

Negli was shooting at anything that moved. Beyond Negli was someone Parker didn't know, and Negli shot at him too and the guy ran behind a cabin.

The guy who killed Ellie? The stupid bastard they'd spent all this time looking for?

It had to be him. At long last, it had to be him.

Parker shouted, "Negli! That's the guy we want!"

Negli fired at his voice, and the ricochet whined on past. Negli shouted, "*You're* the one I want, Parker!"

"What the hell for? What's the matter with you?"

"Arnie's dead, you bastard!"

Negli fired again, but Parker was already gone from there. Keeping one of the cabins between himself and Negli, he moved backward, around the corner of another cabin, and then off to the right. Negli fired again, off at where he used to be, and Parker kept moving to the right.

What did he mean, Arnie was dead? If he was dead, how come? And if he was dead, why was Parker to blame?

Parker moved to the right, around another cabin. There was silence everywhere now. Negli had stopped shooting and started thinking. The question was, which way was he moving? Parker stopped where he was and waited.

Time barely moved. Each second bulged out like a soap

bubble coming out of a kid's bubble pipe, getting bigger and bigger, then suddenly popping and it was time for the next second to start.

For the last couple of days, ever since Ellie was killed and the goods taken, time had been playing tricks like that. Moving fast sometimes, and then inching along other times so an hour took a week or more to be done with.

Last night and today had all been slow, the whole distance. He and Shelly sitting around waiting for Feccio or Clinger or Rudd to phone in with something for them to do. Then every once in a while getting some simpleton to check on, and every time knowing the second he saw the simpleton's face that this wasn't the guy, this couldn't be the guy in a million years. But each time he went on through the complete spiel anyway, while Shelly sat there and looked bored in an easygoing, uncomplaining sort of way. He went through the complete spiel because it was at least something to do while waiting for the right guy to be found.

And gradually he was beginning to wonder if they were going to find him. The guy didn't necessarily have to stay stupid all his life. After missing Parker that second time, up on the roof at Ellie's place, the guy might have smartened up all of a sudden and cleared out of town.

But if he had, they'd still have to find out about it. With Kifka calling people, calling people, building up this list of all the guys Ellie had known, sooner or later their boy's name had to show on that list. And if they went looking for him and couldn't find him home, and everybody else on the list washed out, then at least they'd know the name of the guy they were looking for, and with amateurs you never needed much more than name and general description. Because amateurs work to a pattern, they repeat themselves, they're too comfortable doing the things they've already done before. Amateurs don't like to break new ground, try new patterns.

Given their boy's name and general description, given a few chats with people who knew him, and it wouldn't take long to find out where he'd most likely go with two suitcases full of one hundred thirty-four thousand dollars, or what he'd most likely do once he got there.

He might have to be followed a ways, but he'd eventually be found and the money gotten back.

The only problem was, it was all taking so damn much time. Ellie, for all her laziness and sloppiness, had known a hell of a lot of guys. It took time to get all their names and addresses, time to go looking them up and ask them questions, time to clear them one by one.

That was the kind of time that crept by hamstrung. Like now; waiting in silence for Little Bob Negli to make a mistake, a little guy who's a professional and not in the habit of making mistakes.

And waiting for the amateur to make *his* mistake, a wait that shouldn't take as long.

There was another shot, from up closer to the road, and then two more in rapid succession.

That wouldn't be Negli. That would be the amateur.

The hell with Negli for now. The amateur was the important thing, he couldn't be permitted to get away again. Three times and out; this was the end of the amateur's string.

Parker moved as quickly and as silently as he could around the edge of the cabin and along the grass that flanked the gravel driveway. He kept watching for Negli, looking down every vista between cabins, past the bushes growing against some of the cabins, down toward the pine woods that flanked Vimorama on three sides. He didn't see Negli, not a sign of him, but all at once, ahead of him, he saw the amateur go pelting by, running out of Vimorama entirely, heading for the trees, trying to get away again.

Parker took off after him, jumping across the gravel driveway in two steps, angling through between the cabins to try to head the other one off. Behind him, Negli shouted something he didn't try to understand. A cabin window to his right shattered in time with the sound of a shot from back there. Parker half turned, still running, and snapped a shot in Negli's direction, not to hit him but just to slow him down,

135

distract him. The important thing now was not Negli, it was the goddam amateur.

The amateur went through the woods without looking back, and across the front of a gas station. Parker went after him, running flat out, determined this time not to lose him. And knowing Negli would never be able to keep up to this pace, so he wouldn't have to worry about his back for a while.

Parker was fast, but the amateur was faster, and the gray Ford parked down the road there had to be his. He reached it and flung open the near door, and Parker stopped long enough to put a bullet into the door. He'd been trying for the amateur's leg, but his aim was off because of the running and the lack of time.

But the miss was almost as good as a hit. It deflected the amateur from the car anyway, and sent him off into the woods instead.

Parker got to the car a minute later and looked in and saw the suitcases on the back seat. The same ones. So he'd found the cash at last.

But he couldn't do anything about it yet. There was still the amateur in front of him and Little Bob Negli behind him. Looking down to his left, Parker saw Negli running along on his bantam legs like some sort of silly lunatic from a silent movie comedy, his fancy clothing all rumpled up and torn, the tiny Beretta glinting in his hand, his face dark with thunderclouds.

Which first? If he took the time for Negli, the amateur might be able to circle back and get the car and the loot and take off again. But if he went on after the amateur, why wouldn't Negli do the same thing, just hop into the car and take off after the whole bundle?

No, not Negli. One look at him, running along there like somebody's idea of a joke about vengeance, was enough to tell Parker he didn't have to worry about Negli taking off with the cash. It wasn't cash Negli wanted anymore, it was Parker's scalp. Why he wanted it Parker didn't know, but he could take time to find out later on.

136

The amateur first.

The whole thing, looking into the back seat of the Ford and looking back at Negli and making up his mind which idiot to go after first, the whole thing had taken only a couple of seconds. The amateur could still be heard crashing and blundering through the woods, headed straight away from the road and the car, so scared he wasn't even remembering the cash.

Parker went in after him.

The woods, at first, were like that around Vimorama: well-spaced pine trees with a thick mat of needles covering the ground, darkness and muffled silence, shadows flitting past the black trunks. But the farther they moved from the road, the thicker the going became. Some birch and maple trees began to show up between the pines, clogging the paths more. Dead leaves were mounded around the tree trunks, and the entwined branches of the birches and maples were bare and jagged-looking.

As the pines thinned and the birches and maples increased, more and more bushes began to grow between the trunks. Vines and creepers, roselike bushes covered with thorns, thick rubbery bushes with intertwined branches, clumped hedgelike bushes autumn-stripped of their leaves; they all slowed Parker down, slowed him down.

But they slowed the amateur more. He had to hack and claw his way through the stuff up ahead there, and where he had passed the going was easier for whoever would come through next.

Parker was next, close behind the amateur, moving after him with grim and steady speed. This wasn't going to be like the first time, outside Kifka's place, when night and surprise and a good head start had made it possible for the bastard to get away. Nor like the second time, when the presence of the law there had forced Parker to *help* him get away.

This time it was clear and simple. This time it was straightforward, the way Parker liked it.

The amateur was running, leaving a broad trail. Parker was

following him, and gaining on him. When he caught up with him, he'd kill him.

The land was sloping gradually downward, and now the trees were thinning out and the bushes getting larger and thicker and even harder to fight through. There was still some greenery on some of the underbrush that was green all year round, and here and there bushes sported hard inedible bright red berries, but the color of the forest was mostly black, accented by the white trunks of the birches. Between the trunks swelled the underbrush, sharp and gamy.

Now and again Parker came to clumps of bushes the amateur hadn't been able to go through at all; he could see the marks where the amateur had fought his way part-way in and had then been forced to back out again and go around.

That slowed the amateur too, and helped Parker gain on him.

From time to time Parker caught glimpses of him through the trees and brush; a bobbing head, a straining back. But they were just moving glimpses, and he made no attempt to hit him from this range, given such a bad target. He'd catch up with him sooner or later. The amateur might be faster on open level ground, but not in here.

Parker was so sure that he even stopped at one point and listened for Negli. The little man would be coming along too, he was positive. Being smaller, following this trail after two men bigger than himself had already forced it open, Negli should be able to make fine time in here.

But there was no sound.

Parker frowned and listened. Off the other way, he could hear the amateur still blundering away through the underbrush like a frightened range cow, but back toward the highway there was silence.

The silence was split open by a gunshot. Something thudded into the tree beside Parker's head.

That was the second time Negli's gun had fired off to the right; sooner or later Negli would notice it himself and start compensating.

But he was back there, anyway. Moving more slowly and silently than he had to because he was afraid of being ambushed.

Parker turned and went on after the amateur before Negli had a chance to try for another shot.

He'd lost ground in those few seconds he'd been stopped, but it didn't matter. The end was inevitable anyway.

His topcoat was an annoyance, snagging branches, slowing him down. He stopped again and transferred the pistols to his trouser pockets and stripped off the topcoat. He threw it over a bush and went on.

Abruptly, trees and underbrush stopped. Along a straight line running from left to right there was a sudden border to the forest as clear and neat as though someone had cut the earth with a scissors and in fixing things again had seamed two mismatched parts together at this spot like getting a jigsaw puzzle wrong.

On one side of the seam was the forest, black and red and green, verticaled with birch and maple, jagged-armed at the top, cluttered with underbrush at the bottom. On the other side of the seam was blasted dirt, dry tan in color, so light as to almost be cream. Moisture had eroded and drained from the soil, a few late autumn frosts had done their work, and the ground now was baked and cracked like the surface of the moon. Zigzag lines ran here and there across the powdery dirt. Nothing grew.

Looking up, Parker saw the explanation. In front of him, maybe sixty yards away, a broad yellow brick building rose up in the middle of the dead plain like a squared-off dinosaur. Marching rows of windows reflected the afternoon sun, giving off a cold yellow light. On the right side of the building the temporary steel framework of a construction company's external elevator rose up like the crane next to a missile bound for the moon.

Bulldozers had worked this dry miracle with the land. The constructors of that building over there had called in the bulldozers to strip down every inch of the property they owned before anybody started to work putting up the foundation. Later, when the building was done, landscape architects would come in with fresh earth and seed and hothouse plants and turn this moonscape back into something vaguely like the forest it had been, but with less clutter and liveliness.

The building wasn't finished, that was obvious, though there didn't seem to be any workmen on or near it. Parker assumed they were all out on strike.

Whether the building, when it was finished, would be an apartment house or an office building Parker couldn't tell and didn't care. Whatever it was going to be, it implied a road or highway or street of some kind over on its far side. If the amateur could make it over to there, over to paved street and a populated neighborhood, he just might get away after all.

But he wasn't going to make it.

He was halfway to the building, running splayfooted, arms making ragged pinwheels at his sides. He was obviously winded, running on terror now instead of strength or energy. Little puffs of dust rose up around his feet at every pounding step. He half staggered, nearly fell forward, but kept his balance and his momentum and ran on.

Parker half turned so his right side was to the building and the runner. He stretched his right arm out, shoulder high, large hand bunched around the Colt .38 automatic, arm and hand and automatic all pointing at the straining back of the runner.

He fired.

Dust puffed ahead of the runner and to his right.

The runner didn't dodge, didn't swerve. He kept running straight ahead, flat out, running along the straight taut string of terror.

Parker compensated, aiming now just a bit to the left, just a bit lower. His first finger squeezed and the automatic bucked just a trifle, and the runner thudded face forward into the ground. Dust billowed up around him and slowly settled down again. There was no wind; the dust settled on the body.

Now for Negli.

A bullet cut Parker's right earlobe.

2

There was silence.

Parker crouched next to a thick maple, peering through the underbrush, waiting for Negli to make a move. Behind him, five or six feet away, was the edge of the forest; beyond, the tan earth lay dull and flat, and farther away the yellow building gleamed in the pale sunlight.

It was cold in here now. He'd left his topcoat, and he was no longer moving, and he could feel the chill air seeping through his clothes.

Five minutes had gone by since Negli's bullet had drawn blood on Parker's ear. Parker had taken cover, had moved slowly and carefully away from where Negli could expect to find him, and now he was sitting here and waiting for Negli to make the first move.

It had to be Negli who would move first. He was a pro, the same as Parker, but right now he was running on emotion, and a man full of emotion can't sit and wait as well as a man in control of himself. So Negli would eventually have to move, and when the time came, Parker would take whatever advantage of it he could.

But he wasn't sure yet whether he just wanted to kill Negli or not. If Arnie Feccio really was dead, then there were developments Parker didn't know anything about. For his own good, he had to find out about them, find out how the situation now stood, and Negli was the only one handy to tell him.

The whole operation had soured completely, he knew that much. The job itself, at the stadium, had been sweet, one of the

141

sweetest pieces of work he'd ever been a part of. For three days after the job, everything was still sweet. And then, because of that simple-minded amateur, lying out there now on the dead ground, everything went to hell.

Shelly was dead. If Negli had the story straight, then Feccio was dead, too. Negli was going to be dead himself pretty soon. Three out of the seven, dead or soon to be.

Leaves rattled.

Parker was instantly alert. It had come from the left, and deeper into the woods away from the open ground. Negli had been more to the right earlier, when he'd taken that near-miss shot at Parker. So they'd spent the last five minutes circling each other, both of them moving to the right, shifting position in relation to the forest but not in relation to one another.

If he were to move out to the edge, out by the moonscape, and head down to his left, he might still flank Negli, still wind up on Negli's back. With that advantage, he could pick and choose, he could maybe get close enough just to disarm the little man and hold him down while he asked some questions.

It was worth a try.

He moved to his left, as slow and careful and silent as a wolf.

"Parker!"

He stopped. The call had come from the same spot; Negli hadn't moved since then. Parker said nothing. He waited.

"Parker, you did everything wrong."

He waited.

"You hear me? You stupid lummox, do you hear me?"

He waited.

Negli's voice was getting shrill, his words were bumping into one another. He shouted, "Do you want to hear about it, you brainless bastard?"

This time, as Negli shouted Parker moved. Negli's own roaring voice covered any small sounds Parker might make. He followed the line he'd already worked out, moving out to the edge of the forest and then down the line to get behind Negli. He moved when Negli spoke, and stopped when Negli was silent.

Negli shouted, "You lost the money, that was the *first* thing. You walk out of the apartment and leave the money in there with nobody to watch it and somebody comes and takes it away, you simple moron, takes it *away!*"

Parker stopped. He was at the edge now; he'd traveled about seven feet so far, during Negli's speeches.

It was almost comic. Negli shouting about stupidity and killing himself with every shout.

"And you went to the *cop!*" Negli shouted, and Parker moved forward again. "You got that goddam list from that goddam cop, and what the hell did you *think* he'd do? You hear me, Parker? What did you *think* that cop would do?"

They both stopped.

"He put law on the *inside*, Parker! There weren't any cops watching for *you* on the *outside*, there were plainclothesmen inside the goddam apartment!"

Parker frowned and crouched down to wait awhile. That was a cross-up. It didn't make sense that way. Detective Dougherty had to figure he was part of the mob that made the haul at the stadium. He had to figure Parker would lead him to the rest of the mob. It only made sense for Dougherty to put men on watch *outside* the homes of those nine men on his list with orders not to grab Parker when he showed up but to follow him when he left.

That was the whole basis of it right there, that was why it seemed safe to let the others go around and ask their questions.

Why? Where had he figured wrong? Had Dougherty been too smart for him or too dumb for him?

Negli shouted again: "They put the grab on Arnie, you know that? I saw them bring him out. I tried to help him cop it, they gunned him down. *You hear me, you rotten bastard?*"

Parker heard him. He'd gone down the line now, Negli's voice was coming from farther back. He'd managed to cross Negli's flank and get behind him. He turned, and on Negli's next speech he started in through the underbrush again.

"*Parker!* Arnie's *dead!* Don't you know what I'm talking about, you mindless piece of hate? Arnie's *dead!*"

Closer, Parker stopped, his left hand resting lightly on the smooth white trunk of a birch tree. The automatic was in his right. The little Colt revolver was still in his trouser pocket, hadn't been used at all yet.

"And that other one! He killed Kifka, did you know that? Not just your girl, that slut of yours, you animal, not just her. He killed Kifka, too, just now, just today."

Kifka? Then who was left?

Shelly dead, Feccio dead, Negli dying. Kifka dead. If the law was on watch inside those apartments, then they now must have Clinger and Rudd.

Nobody was left.

Only Parker was left. Parker, and a corpse that was shouting because it didn't know yet it was a corpse.

"Kifka's your fault, too, Parker, you hear that? You killed Arnie just as much as if you pulled the trigger yourself. *You* killed Arnie, and you killed Kifka, and *I'm* going to kill you!"

They stopped. Negli was no more than ten feet away now, ahead and to the right. Crouching, waiting, Parker peered through the underbrush for some sign, some glimpse of Negli. He'd been wearing a luminous tan camel's hair coat over his natty suit; that tan should show nicely against the black and green of the woods. But not yet, not quite close enough yet.

The wait this time was a longer one, and when at last Negli spoke out again there was a difference in the tone of his voice. He seemed suddenly less full of rage, less sure of himself:

"Parker? Parker? Where the hell are you, Parker?"

A foot closer. Two feet closer.

"Did you run away, you bastard? You coward? You moron?"
Closer.

"Why don't you fight like a *man?*"

There was a sudden scattering of leaves, and Negli was standing up in full sight, staring and staring the wrong way, his natty back to Parker and only five feet away.

"Why don't you fight like a *man!*"

Parker shot him in the back of the head.

144

3

There was law all over the car.

Parker stood there, just within the cover of the pine trees, looking out at the gray Ford. He saw Dougherty there, and another plainclothesman, and three or four cops in uniform.

After he'd finished with Negli he'd worked his way back here along the path he and the other two had beaten out. He'd gathered up his topcoat from where he'd thrown it and put it back on, and when he worked his way up out of the thick underbrush and the birch and maple trees and in under the cool, dim spaciousness of the pine trees he took time out to brush himself off, rub away the dirt marks and the grass stains, get himself looking a little more sensible and civilized. He buried the two pistols under some loose dirt and pine needles because he wouldn't be needing them any more and went on through the pines and almost stepped out into the open before he saw the law all over the car.

He'd taken too long. If it had just been the amateur everything would have been all right, but with the extra time it had taken to deal with Negli he'd stretched beyond the limit.

Five minutes sooner and he'd have been free and clear, with wheels and the whole boodle.

But there was no chance for it now. As he stood in among the trees and watched, Dougherty and the other plainclothesman reached into the Ford and took out one of the suitcases and set it down on the ground next to the car. They looked at one another, and then both crouched down in front of the suitcase and loosened the snaps. The other plainclothesman lifted the lid.

145

The money was stacked in there like heads of lettuce.

Both cops stood up again and put their hands on their hips and looked down at the open suitcase. Then Dougherty turned his head and looked at the woods in the general direction of Parker. He said something to the other cop, but Parker was too far away to hear the words. The other cop looked at the woods too and shook his head. Dougherty shrugged.

Parker waited a minute longer even though there wasn't any point to it. He watched the cops take out a second suitcase, not one of the right ones, and open it up to find it full of laundry. Then they reached in again and this time brought out the right suitcase, and then they had both suitcases and all the money, and it was all over.

Never had such a sweet operation turned so completely sour.

Of the seven in on the job, all but one were dead or in the hands of the law. The take was in the hands of the law. There was nothing left.

Parker turned away and started back through the forest again.

The only thing to do now was get clear. The job was so completely sour, it was a kind of victory just to get himself out and clear.

The best way was the way the amateur had tried. Through the forest and out past that building under construction and along whatever street or road there was on the other side of it. Not back into town at all after that, but the other way, farther out of the city.

He had a little money on him, not much. Enough to carry him away from here.

He paused for a second where he'd buried the guns. But he'd be better off without them. From here on, what he had to do was keep out of sight. Gun battles with the law were for idiots.

He moved on, following the same trail as last time. But this time there was no one ahead of him and no one coming along behind him.

Back in the other direction, the sun crept down behind the pine trees. Darkness was slowly edging in from all sides, but there was still enough light to see the trail.

4

The amateur was gone.

Parker stopped at the edge of the woods, peering, at first refusing to believe it, telling himself he was being tricked by perspective, by the long forest shadows that stretched now like witch fingers out across the dead plain toward the building, by the bad light of late afternoon.

But it was no trick. Where the amateur had fallen, where the dust had billowed up and then settled on him again, there was now no one. No one and nothing.

The second bullet hadn't done the job, then. It had seemed like a good hit, but it had only wounded him. And he'd lain out there, either lying doggo or unconscious, and after a while he'd crawled or walked away.

Which way? Back into the relative safety of the woods? Or forward, on toward that building bulking out there?

Forward. There was no subtlety in the amateur, nothing in him but direct action. He would keep going forward no matter what.

But there were still questions. It all depended how badly he was hit. From the way he'd flopped out there, from how long he'd stayed lying there, the hit had to be fairly good, anyway. It was no flesh wound, no grazing of his shoulder or leg. But just how bad was it? Bad enough to have him dead now, up closer to the building? Or not quite that bad, but bad enough to force him to hole up in the building itself and not try to go any farther? Or was it so slight after all that he'd just walked away and was now lost forever?

Standing there at the edge of the woods, Parker regretted not having dug the guns up again. But there'd been no way to guess back there that he'd be needing a gun again so soon.

He faded back into the woods, hunted around, and found the body of Negli lying sprawled all over a thick and thorny bush. The little Beretta was on the ground near his hand.

Parker picked it up and broke the clip out of the butt. It was a six-shot .25-caliber automatic, and Negli had already used up five of the cartridges in this clip.

Parker slid the clip back in place, put the Beretta in his pocket, and dragged Negli clear of the thornbush. He went through Negli's clothing, but the little man hadn't been carrying an extra clip.

The damn fool!

Parker got to his feet and looked out again across the plain at the building over there. It was over twenty stories high already, and from the confusion of cranes and pulleys atop the building—looking like unruly hair on the head of a Mongoloid idiot—it was apparently going to be even taller before they were done. The last rays of sunlight glinted like icicles from the windows on the first seven or eight floors; above that the windowpanes hadn't been put in place yet.

The amateur might be in there. He might be anywhere inside that pile of brick and glass, or he might be gone from this area entirely.

Parker wanted him. He wanted that bastard the way Negli had wanted Parker. Not because there was any sense in it anymore, but only because the amateur, alive, was a loose end.

It was the amateur who had soured the sweet job, bringing in his own extraneous problems, killing for no sensible reason, taking money that should have been safe, running around wild and causing trouble with everybody, attracting the attention of the law.

There was no profit in killing him, but Parker was going to kill him anyway. He was going to kill him because he couldn't possibly just walk away and leave the bastard alive.

But that didn't mean he had to get like Negli, stupid and careless.

148

It would be full night soon, and that was bad. Night was the amateur's ally, covering his blunders, obstructing Parker's movements. If the thing was to be done, it should be done now.

He moved out across the dead plain, moving light and fast on the balls of his feet, watching the building, ready to jump in any direction. If the amateur was in there, and watching, and waiting for a good shot, that was all right. Parker would give him one shot to find out exactly where he was. He could count on the bastard to miss the first time.

But there was no shot. He came all the way across the plain and up to the building itself and there was no sound, no movement.

This was the back of the building. Windows stretched away to left and right, reflecting with distortions the plain and the forest and the red circle of the sun beginning now to sink behind the western horizon. A few gray metal doors were snugly in place here and there along the rear wall, implying basements, furnaces, all the utilities needed for a bulging building like this one.

No sound, no movement.

But over to the right a window was smashed in. These were all permanent windows, fixed in place without any way to open them, meaning the building would be centrally air-conditioned. Over to the right, one of these windows had been smashed in, and every last piece of glass knocked out of the aluminum frame.

So a man could crawl through without cutting himself.

A sound, a tiny scratch, made him look up.

Glinting like a phantom airship, slender, square, fast and murderous, a sheet of plate glass knifed down through the air at him, whistling. Highlights sparkled from the edges like reflections of ice.

Parker jumped away. With a sound like dry wood breaking, only much much louder, the sheet of glass destroyed itself into the ground, spraying shards and slivers in all directions. Silver triangles tinkled against the ground floor windows. Tiny

149

pyramids of glass embedded themselves in Parker's shin and cheek and the back of his right hand.

He looked up; the wall loomed up featureless and blank, the glass blood-red in the windows on the lower floors, reflecting the sun. The yellow bricks of the wall were tinged with rose color.

The amateur was up there, on a high story, above the levels where the glass had already been fixed in place.

As Parker looked, a dusky shimmer extruded from high up the wall like the phantom of a slender tongue. It bent, it arched, it broke free of the wall and sliced downward; another heavy sheet of glass, three feet wide and four feet long and half an inch thick, slicing through the air like an invisible sword.

Parker dove through the hole in the building where the amateur had already smashed a window in. Behind him, the second glass torpedo sprayed itself into oblivion, musically.

He was in what would be a basement storage room, the interior walls made of concrete block and painted a dull blue-gray. A metal door stood open onto a concrete block corridor.

Parker moved cautiously, the Beretta insignificant in his hand. The corridor led him to the left to gaping holes in the wall where some day the elevators would hang. Opposite, another metal door led him to a stairway, the rough plaster walls painted an unfortunate yellow. He took the stairs up to the first floor.

He was now in what would be a lobby or entrance hall of some kind, a broad, dim, white-painted echoing cavern with a low-hung free-form ceiling, shaped like a swimming-pool Light fixtures sprouted all over this ceiling like the faceted eyes of flies.

From here on, every part of the building was incomplete. A metal staircase, without the walls that would enclose it, stood off to the left, leading upward. Parker went that way, sliding his feet noiselessly across a floor that seemed to be, but was not, marble.

Beside the staircase a white bag fell and exploded, puffing

whiteness out everywhere. A bag of cement, dropped too early.

Parker ran through it, a white mist like a smokescreen in wartime, and started up the stairs. The stairs went forward to a landing, backward to the second floor. Forward again to another landing, backward to the third floor. And so on, and so on. And between the stairway halves was an empty space running down the middle of the stairwell, down which, like down some madman's oubliette, the amateur hurled whatever he could get his hands on. Long warped one-by-twelve planks went bumping and thumping by, bouncing from metal railing to metal railing. More cement bags dropped by like torsos to make soft white explosions on the lobby floor. Hammers and wrenches fell by, rattling and clanking.

Parker kept to the far edge of the stairs, and kept moving upward. The windows had been glassed in completely up to the eighth floor. More than two or three floors above that there probably wasn't even any glass in readiness yet, lying around to be used as weapons. On floor nine, then, or floor ten or floor eleven he would find the amateur.

As he passed the sixth-floor level the rain of stupidity stopped from above. The amateur had been throwing out of fear, out of panic, and now either his panic had abated or he had run out of things to throw.

Why hadn't he used his gun? Was he out of bullets, or had he lost the gun somewhere, or was he just too panic-struck to remember he had it?

The silence after the crash and clatter seemed to hum with emptiness. Parker moved more slowly, listening, listening through the silence, and wasn't surprised after a minute to hear the hurried stealthy scuffing of feet on stairs. The amateur was climbing higher.

Parker was in no hurry. After the fifth floor, there were hardly any interior partitions up at all, and he could see there was no other way to go up or down but this stairwell. As long as he was below the amateur, and controlled the stairwell, there was no hurry.

Except the press of darkness. Half the sun had now

disappeared below the horizon, and the top half glowered winter-red, tinging glass and plaster and metal with rose and saffron.

The sounds that came from above were like the sounds of mice in walls, but they were made by the amateur creeping up the metal stairs on hands and knees, wincing and grimacing, trying desperately and vainly to be silent. Parker could visualize him from the sounds and moved more openly himself now, not worrying so much about noise.

At the landing between the tenth and eleventh floors, set carefully and symmetrically in the middle of the floor, there was a little mound of money.

Parker stared at it. It was an offering, a sacrifice, like some South Sea Islander giving his virgin daughter to a volcano. The little mound of money left on the landing like an offertory on an altar.

Parker picked it up and counted it. There were forty twenty-dollar bills and eight ten-dollar bills: eight hundred eighty dollars.

He had some of the money!

Parker looked upward. The bastard hadn't left all the money in the suitcases; he'd taken some of it with him, he had it on his person. And not just this much, just eight hundred eighty dollars. There'd be more of it.

Parker stuffed the sacrifice in his pocket and went more quickly up the stairs. It was now necessary to keep the amateur from falling or jumping, to keep him in a condition where his pockets could be searched.

And all with extreme care. There was only one bullet left in the Beretta, and that only .25 caliber and a very short-barreled gun.

The amateur might jump, if he was terrified enough. Or fall, because of stupidity.

Noises again, six or seven flights up. Parker, at the fourteenth story, stopped to listen. Scrapings, thumpings, heavy sounds. But nothing coming down the stairwell, nothing immediate.

152

The noises went on and on as Parker kept climbing, and stopped as he was rounding the landing above the eighteenth story. He went two more flights and saw above him what the amateur had done.

A barricade. Strips of metal, bundles of wire, planks of wood, tools of all kinds, even a wheelbarrow, all piled and jumbled together at the head of the stairs to keep him down.

And was the barricade defended? Was this where the amateur would make his last stand?

No. Waiting on the landing below, just out of range if the amateur were armed and manning the barricade, Parker listened and once again heard the mouse noises farther up. The amateur was still running.

Parker went on up and brushed through the barricade with impatient arms. Tools and planks and bundles went crashing away, some clattering down the stairs, and up above the amateur cried out at the noise.

Above the twenty-first floor, there weren't even external walls any more, only the flat white outlines of the poured concrete foundation. Floor and ceiling were rudimentary here: a thick flat slab of concrete swarming underneath with rods and cables and wires and other projections growing out like hair. Going forward from floor to landing, there was nothing beyond the left edge of each stair but emptiness and the setting sun and the dead plain far below. No banister, no railing, nothing. Going the other half, from landing to floor, there was nothing to the right of each stair but that other half of staircase hanging out over emptiness.

The amateur was only one flight away, creeping upward, trembling, making more and more noise. He was gasping for breath and groaning from a thousand terrors. Parker followed, keeping to the middle of each stair, looking only at the stairs and his own feet, moving upward.

The twenty-third floor was the top. The flooring here was planks, covering only parts of the area and leaving other parts open. Wooden forms for the concrete foundation jutted up here and there like Renaissance smoke-stacks. Olive-drab tarpaulins were thrown over mounds of material.

Across the way, the framework of the construction elevator stood like a model of the Eiffel Tower. The elevator itself, a mesh cage, hung within it at the level of this floor. The amateur was making for it, hobbling, running crouched like a wounded bear. He wore a dirty cream-colored raincoat, the back all stained and darkened by blood. He was torso-hit, just above the waist on the left side of the back.

Exerting himself the way he was, hit like that with the bullet certainly still in him, he was done anyway. He was big and strong—Parker remembered how the sword had been thrust entirely through Ellie and into the wall behind—and if he'd had only a normal share of strength he'd be finished already. The end was coming soon. If it weren't for the money, Parker could just go away and leave him up here to rot.

But there was the money. Parker walked across the echoing planks.

The amateur wrenched open the two gates and stumbled into the elevator. Turning, he saw Parker and cried out again as he had before. He pushed the gates shut and tried to work the lever to send the elevator down to the ground, but of course there wasn't any power. The construction company people had sent the elevator to the top of the shaft before leaving so stray kids wouldn't damage it and then had turned the power off and gone away.

The amateur had caged himself.

Parker walked across the planks toward him.

The amateur wrenched open the two gates.

The amateur shouted, "Don't shoot at me! Please don't shoot at me!"

There was an open space at the top of the double gate across the front of the elevator. The amateur with a sudden motion threw something over this, something that landed hard on the planks, and bounced: a stubby black pistol.

"I lost the other one!" he shouted. Parker was close to him now, but he kept shouting anyway, as though he thought there was some sort of wall between himself and Parker. "I'm not armed now!" he shouted. "There's my gun! There's my gun!"

Parker walked up to the front of the cage. He had the Beretta in his right hand, but at the last second he changed his mind. He went back and picked up the gun the amateur had thrown away; it was a Smith & Wesson .32 revolver. Parker frowned at it. The last one like this he'd seen, Pete Rudd was carrying it. Was this Rudd's pistol? Was that how the amateur knew to come to Vimorama?

But he wasn't particularly interested in the answer, because it made no difference anymore. He turned back to the man in the cage.

"Don't shoot at me, please. She did deserve that; you knew her, you must have known she deserved it, and I never meant to cause you any trouble, it all just happened one thing after the other, all I wanted to do was give her what she—"

Parker used one bullet from Pete Rudd's gun.

He pulled open the gates and went in and rolled the amateur over on his back and went through his pockets.

Left trouser pocket, sixty-three twenties. Right trouser pocket, thirty-nine twenties and twenty-five tens. Left hip pocket, fifty-two tens and ten fifties. Right hip pocket, forty-seven twenties and nine tens and eight fifties. Right shirt pocket, forty-two twenties and four hundreds. Nothing in the left shirt pocket; that must have been where the eight hundred eighty bucks had come from.

Still more. Left jacket pocket, fifty twenties and nine fifties. Right jacket pocket, fifty-three twenties and seven fifties. Inside jacket pocket, ninety-five twenties and three hundreds.

The amateur had bulged with cash, bloated with cash, overflowed with cash.

Left raincoat pocket, ninety-three twenties and seventeen tens. Right raincoat pocket, eighty twenties and fifteen fifties.

All together, seven hundreds and forty-nine fifties and six hundred two twenties and one hundred eleven tens, including the money left on the stairs.

Sixteen thousand three hundred dollars.